# THE BOSS'S FAKE FIANCÉE

BY

SUSAN MEIER

MILLS & BOON

First published in Great Britain 2017
By Mills & Boon, an imprint of HarperCollins*Publishers*
1 London Bridge Street, London, SE1 9GF

Large Print edition 2017

© 2017 Linda Susan Meier

ISBN: 978-0-263-07172-6

**MIX**
Paper from
responsible sources
FSC
www.fsc.org  **FSC™ C007454**

This book is produced from independently certified FSC paper to ensure responsible forest management. For more information visit www.harpercollins.co.uk/green.

Printed and bound in Great Britain
by CPI Group (UK) Ltd, Croydon, CR0 4YY

X

# THE BOSS'S
# FAKE FIANCÉE

# CHAPTER ONE

"I THINK YOU'RE going to have to do more than show up at the wedding."

Mitcham Ochoa tossed his pen to his desk and glared at his cousin Riccardo. It wasn't exactly like looking in a mirror when he saw Riccardo, but it was close. All the Ochoa men had dark hair and dark eyes. Most were tall. The same age, Mitch and Riccardo didn't just share physical characteristics; they behaved like brothers and knew everything there was to know about each other. Both had also been dumped by a woman they thought they wanted to marry. Except Riccardo had been broken to his very core when his fiancée chose her former boyfriend over him and Mitch eventually realized he hadn't really loved Julia. Because Riccardo knew that, Mitch was not pleased with what Riccardo was hinting.

"I'm over her."

Riccardo winced. "You know that and I know that, but it isn't every day that a woman leaves her boyfriend for his brother, and then the jilted brother is asked to be the best man at their wedding. Tongues are going to wag, my friend. Everybody's going to watch every move you make. Unless—"

"Unless what?"

"Unless you have no reason to be jealous."

Righteous indignation whipped through Mitch and he bounced out of his tall-back black leather office chair. If anybody knew Mitch felt nothing but happiness for his brother and Julia, it was Riccardo. It annoyed the hell out of him that his cousin was pushing this nonissue. "I have no reason to be jealous!"

"Your brother is the oldest. He got the CEO-ship of your family's business. He stole your girlfriend."

Mitch growled.

"And let's face it. He's better looking."

Mitch tossed his pen at Riccardo, who ducked.

"It's reactions like that that will have Nanna fussing over you for the two weeks we're in Spain celebrating this wedding. Do you want to have Nanna hovering?"

Finally seeing what Riccardo was doing, he slowly lowered himself to his seat again. "No." Oh, Lord. He did not want Nanna hovering. His mother would be bad enough, but his grandmother? If she thought he was having even one iota of sadness over Julia marrying his brother, she'd do everything but spoon-feed him his dessert and make him look pathetic, when he wasn't. Finding his brother in his bedroom with his girlfriend two years ago hadn't been upsetting as much as it had been a wake-up call that rippled through his whole life. Losing Julia had put him back into the dating pool where he'd realized maybe their "love" was more about convenience than real emotion. They'd been together so long that staying together just seemed like the right thing to do. Recognizing the mistake he'd almost made in the name of comfort had jarred him. And now he was smarter, sharper, alert to the pitfalls of getting too comfortable with anything.

"Then you have to figure out a way to prove— from the very second you step off the Ochoa Vineyards jet—that you're not just fine with this wedding. You are happy."

Unfortunately, his family didn't seem to see that his brother's betrayal hadn't really been a betrayal but a way for Mitch to dodge a big, fat bullet. They didn't see how it had spring-boarded him to the kind of success he'd always longed for. All they remembered was that the initial shock of it had thrown Mitch into a tailspin. This was what he got for moving an ocean away. They hadn't seen how quickly he'd bounced back. And when he tried to tell them, they thought he was either attempting to smooth things over or save face.

"The only way Nanna will ever think I'm happy is if I'm married."

Riccardo frowned. "You can't get married before your brother. No time." He stopped. His face shifted and he burst out laughing. "But you could bring a fiancée to the wedding celebrations."

"Right."

"No! I'm serious! All you have to do is find a woman to agree to be your fiancée for the two weeks we're in Spain. You make up a story about how you met. You create some romantic schmaltzy thing about how you proposed. You kiss her a few times in front of Nanna and—" He snapped his fingers. "You're no longer the rejected brother."

"Except I'm engaged?"

"No. No. A couple weeks later, you call Nanna. You say you had a fight and you're not engaged anymore. And you don't really have to explain too much until the next time you go home."

He had to admit there was a certain poetry to it. He'd sneaked home to propose to Julia the night he'd found her and his brother in the bedroom of their apartment. They were fully clothed, but there weren't a whole hell of a lot of reasons why Alonzo would be in her bedroom, except that they were lovers. Alonzo had vehemently denied it. He'd even told Mitch he'd walked in on their first kiss. They weren't cheating. They didn't want to hurt him. But it was clear from the way Alonzo protected Julia that Mitch's brother might not be sleeping with her, but he loved her.

He'd been gobsmacked, but the whole mess had prompted his dad to give him the go-ahead to start the project he'd been angling to try for years: put his family's wines online. He'd moved to New York for a change of scenery and grown to love the city. He'd also gotten so good at selling his family's wines that he'd started a second website. That site sold wines from numerous vineyards—and glasses, wine racks, corkscrews, aprons, T-shirts with funny wine sayings, books on wine, books on serving wine, books on hosting wine-tasting parties—anything and everything related to wines. That was the site where he made money. Lots of money. Enough money to bring Riccardo from Spain to New York to help him start three more specialty websites. One sold anything and everything to do with cycling. One sold cooking supplies. One sold anything to do with golf.

All he had to do was pick a topic, find the vendors who made the "best" of whatever he wanted to sell, test their products, rule out the weak, choose the good and create a site. There was enough variety in the duties that he was never bored, and Riccardo was a financial genius. Whatever money Mitch's websites brought in was invested to make more money. Though they wouldn't tell their family, they were on track to be worth more than the entire Ochoa family enterprises in as few as three years.

So losing Julia had opened the door for him to become the businessman he was today. The very fact that he wouldn't go back and change the outcome was proof that everything that had happened was for his benefit.

Still, none of those things would sway Nanna into believing he was happy, and she'd more than hover. She'd make him look pathetic. Worse, his grandmother making a big deal about him would put a real damper on his brother's wedding. This was supposed to be Julia and Alonzo's special time, two weeks of celebrating, and if he didn't do something, his presence could actually ruin it.

But if he didn't attend the wedding, refused to

be best man, people would gossip that he was upset and the whole wedding would be about him not being there.

Either way, Julia and Alonzo's wedding could become all about him.

He had to fix this.

"So where do we find this woman who'd be willing to pretend to be my fiancée for two weeks?"

Lila Ross gathered the sheets of paper that flew out of the copier, stacked them neatly, stapled them and headed into her boss's office. It wasn't often that she had both Mitch and Riccardo in the same room at the same time. She had to take advantage of this opportunity to get their approval on last month's income statements, especially since they were leaving the next day for a family wedding.

Reports ready, she shoved her big-frame glasses up her nose and headed for the open door. She knocked twice to let them know she was there, then entered the room talking.

"I have last month's income statements."

Mitch said, "Great. Thanks. Come in."

Riccardo's face shifted. His eyes narrowed. His forehead wrinkled. His head tilted.

Deciding that expression probably had something to do with whatever they'd been discussing before she came in and was, therefore, none of her business, she handed one of the reports to Mitch and one to Riccardo before she sat on the empty chair in front of Mitch's huge chrome-and-glass desk. The floor-to-ceiling windows behind Mitch displayed a beautiful view of the Manhattan skyline, glittering in the bright sunlight of a perfect June morning. The big geometric print area rug beneath her feet protected hardwood floors bleached then stained a medium gray that complemented the gray paint on the walls. The ultramodern black sofa and chair sat with a chrome-and-glass coffee table and end tables that matched the desk. The room was the picture of luxury and success that didn't surprise her. Mitch Ochoa had the Midas touch.

Not to mention good looks and charm.

He glanced up at her and smiled. "Give me two minutes to peruse this, and then we'll talk specifics."

Her heart pitter-pattered. When he smiled, it was like the sun breaking over the horizon in her soul. "Sure."

He smiled again before he began reading.

She told herself not to look at his shiny black hair as he read, but that only took her eyes to his broad shoulders, white shirt and black tie. He was so urbane. Born and raised in Spain, he'd been all over Europe before he'd come to the United States. She had no idea why he'd chosen New York City to start his breakaway business, but every night she'd thanked her lucky stars that he had—

Every night until last night.

Last night, she'd finally realized that she'd been his assistant for an entire year. They'd eaten many a lunch together. Not to mention late-night dinners when they worked until midnight to get something online or to wait for stats at the end of a new product day.

He could have kissed her thirty-seven times. She'd counted.

But while she'd gazed up at him with stars in her eyes, he'd looked down at her with the eyes of a friend. No. Scratch that. He'd looked down at an assistant. She hadn't even broken the barrier to become his friend.

And last night—

She fought the urge to squeeze her eyes shut as pain and emptiness assaulted her.

Last night, she'd realized he would never see her as anything other than an employee, and she had to start job hunting. As long as she was this close to him day after day, she would continue believing that someday he'd notice her. But if he hadn't noticed her—not even as a friend—after an entire year of late nights and weekends, he wouldn't *ever* notice her. It was time to get on with her life.

And if she really wanted to get on with her life, she had to find a job with a company where she could climb the corporate ladder and eventually earn enough money that she could start looking for her birth mom. They'd been separated when she was ten. Raised in a series of foster homes, she'd been without a family, a place, since then. Finding her birth mom would give her the sense of belonging she'd always yearned for. That meant she had to get away from the distraction of Mitcham Ochoa.

Riccardo cleared his throat. "These numbers look fine, Mitch." He tossed his copy of the income statement to Mitch's desk. "So maybe we can finish talking about that thing we were discussing before Lila came in."

Mitch's head jerked up. His gaze flew to his cousin, then over to Lila and back to Riccardo again, as if reminding Riccardo they had an employee in the room. "Now?"

"I just want you to see the opportunity you have before you. We were talking about not being able to find a certain person to fulfill a specific job, and suddenly I'm thinking perhaps that person is right under our noses."

Okay. She wasn't stupid. They were talking about her. If she was reading this situation correctly, they had a job they needed to fill and she fit the bill. For Mitch to be cautious, the new job had to be a promotion.

Her heart leaped with joy. A promotion would mean more money—maybe enough to hire a private investigator to begin searching for her mom—

Then she remembered that for her sanity and her future, she had to leave Mitch Ochoa's employ and her heart sank. Wasn't it just like fate to finally give her a chance at a promotion when she'd decided—firmly decided—it was time to move on? As hard as she'd worked to climb the ladder in this growing company, she also knew herself. Other people might think she simply had a crush on Mitch. But she couldn't work for someone for a year without getting to know him. In her heart, she genuinely loved him. And promotion or not, she had to leave this job or she'd end up living her life for a man who barely noticed her. Then even if she found her mom, she'd be a broke, single spinster. Not a mom. Not a wife. Not a woman who gave her mom grandkids. She'd be none of the things she longed to be.

She rose from her seat. "I'm not a hundred percent sure what you're talking about, but I think I should tell you that I—"

Riccardo held up a finger to stop her. "No decisions until you hear us out."

Mitch said, "Riccardo," his voice a warning growl.

Riccardo walked behind Lila's chair, put his hands on her shoulders and sat her down again. In two quick moves, he had her chopstick-like pins out of her chestnut-brown hair, and it fell to her shoulders in a curly waterfall. Then he reached forward and removed her glasses.

If Mitch had done either of those, she probably would have swooned at his touch. Because it was all-business Riccardo, she spun around and gaped at him. "What are you doing?"

He turned her head to face front. "Are you seeing what I'm seeing?"

Mitch blinked. "Oh, my God. Yes."

"*Sí*. She is perfect."

Mitch rose and rounded his desk to lean against it, in front of her. "Pale and delicate to Julia's dark features."

"Short and petite where Julia's a little taller."

"Smart," Mitch added.

Riccardo laughed. "I won't insult Julia by making the obvious comparison."

Lila looked from Mitch to Riccardo and back to Mitch again. "What comparison? And could I have my glasses back so I can see?"

Riccardo said, "You can't see without your glasses?"

She took her thick glasses from his hand. "Why else would anyone wear them?"

"Do you have contacts?" Mitch asked quietly, seriously.

Their gazes met and she swallowed hard. For the first time in a year, he wasn't looking at her as an assistant but as a woman. She wasn't sure how she knew the difference, except something in his eyes had shifted, changed, and a million fireflies glowed in her stomach.

"Yes. I have contacts. But I only wear them for special occasions."

Riccardo said, "We have a very special occasion for you."

"You're sending me somewhere?"

"*I'm* taking you somewhere."

Oh, wow. The only thing she'd heard in that sentence was *I'm taking you*. Her heart about popped out of her chest, and she knew she was in more trouble than she'd even believed the night before. She had to get away from this man or she'd be knitting sweaters for him when he was eighty as he dated twenty-year-old starlets.

"Mitch's brother is getting married," Riccardo said. "In Spain."

She frowned. "I know. I reserved the family jet for you guys."

"Yeah, well, Mitch needs more help than reserving the jet."

Mitch pushed away from the desk. "You know what? I think Lila and I should talk about this privately."

Riccardo's eyebrows rose in question.

Mitch said, "Think it through, Riccardo. The less you know, the better the ruse will work."

Riccardo laughed. "Okay. I get it." He scooped up his copy of the income statement. "I'll be in my office, but just remember I'm your detail guy. You won't want to leave me out of the loop completely."

He left the room, but in the last second, reached in, grabbed the knob on the door to the office and closed it.

The oddest feeling snaked through Lila. She'd been alone with Mitch a million times, behind closed doors lots of those times. But suddenly it felt like everything had changed.

"I really do need a favor. A big favor," Mitch said, walking around his desk and dropping into his black leather chair.

"How big?" Seriously? Had her voice just shivered? The man was not the Big Bad Wolf and she certainly wasn't Little Red Riding Hood. She'd been a foster child until she was eighteen. She'd fended for herself forever. Even in some ugly situations. How could a man she'd known a year, a

man she loved and respected, send that kind of
fear skittering through her?

"Riccardo already mentioned that my brother
is getting married."

"Yes."

He leaned back in his chair. "What you don't
know is that Alonzo's fiancée had been my girlfriend." He glanced up, caught her gaze. "I cut a
business trip short, sneaked into our apartment to
surprise her with an engagement ring and caught
them together in our bedroom."

Her eyes widened. "Yikes."

He waved his hands. "They were fully clothed.
But, really? What reason did my brother have
being so comfortable in my bedroom with the
woman I'd come home to propose to?"

"None."

"Exactly. They had the good graces not to even
try to deny that they'd taken advantage of my
many trips for our family's vineyard to…get to
know each other."

She couldn't help it. She giggled. He had such
a sense of humor. And he seemed fine with his
brother's betrayal—or was it his girlfriend's be-

trayal? Oh, God. It was both. How had he gotten over that? Maybe she shouldn't have laughed?

He sat up. "That's exactly the attitude I'd want you to have. That my brother marrying my former girlfriend is no big deal. Funny even. Because I couldn't be happier for them. Alonzo truly loves Julia. She truly loves him. Theirs is the match that should have been made all along."

Putting some of this together in her analytical brain, she said, "So you want me to come to Spain with you?"

*"Sí."*

"As your date for the wedding." The very thought made her nerve endings do a happy dance, but she told them to settle down. There was no way she could agree to that.

"No. Actually, I'd want you to pretend to be my fiancée."

Her breathing stopped. "What?"

"My mom is okay. She has a lot of duties with the wedding to keep her busy. But my grandmother? She's got way too much free time. I swear to God," he said, raising his hands and opening them in supplication, "it won't matter what I say. She'll treat me like a wounded puppy the entire celebration."

"And everybody will feel sorry for you."

"It's not just about pride. It's about Julia and Alonzo's special celebration. I don't want the focus to be on me. I want it on them."

"True."

He leaned a little farther back in his chair. "I turned this arm of my family's enterprise into our company's biggest moneymaker. I'm branching out on my own. I don't want to spend two weeks with my dad looking at me as if I'm emotionally unstable and wondering if he should replace me, even though I'm making tons of money for him and even more money for myself."

"Never thought of that."

"Then you don't know how stubborn and thick-headed Spanish men can be."

*Oh, she had a pretty good idea.*

"Your presence alone will satisfy everybody's curiosity about how I dealt with my brother moving in on my girlfriend while I was traveling." He laughed. "Or maybe I should say just your presence will prove that I easily handled my brother and girlfriend falling in love. And there will be no talk, no questions. Discussions with my dad will go smoothly. My grandmother will chat you up about our future wedding plans and probably take you shopping for china patterns, not smother me with unwanted, unnecessary sympathy."

He took a breath, then added, "I'm not going to lie. This will be a long two weeks of acting for you. But I'll compensate you. In fact, right now I'm so sure this is the best way to go that I'm willing to give you anything you want."

*What she wanted was him.*

But that was actually what made this favor impossible. "I can't." She'd get stars in her eyes. She'd read into things and when she came home she'd be even more in love with him than she was now. So, no. She couldn't do it.

"Okay, let me be frank. The family jet leaves tomorrow. I can't go out and hunt up a woman to do this for me. Not someone whose discretion I trust. Because you truly have to keep this secret. If my family even suspects this is a ruse, it will backfire." He held her gaze. "I trust you in a way I've never trusted anyone. And I need you. I honestly don't think anybody but you could pull this off."

She said nothing, torn between agreeing simply because she was an employee who believed it was her job to do whatever her boss wanted, and recognizing this wasn't a normal boss/assistant request. It was above and beyond her duties. And potentially heartbreaking for her.

"Isn't there anything you want?"

She said nothing.

"Anything you need?"

That's when it hit her. She did have something she needed. She could ask him to use his considerable resources to find her mom, but then she'd still be working for him. She'd spend two weeks pretending to be his fiancée and come home to being his assistant again. That was a heartbreak waiting to happen.

But a new job would not only provide money for a private investigator to locate her mom, it would get her away from Mitch and her pointless crush. She really would be getting a fresh start.

"I need a new job."

He frowned. "What?"

"I want a new job." Assistant jobs, though a dime a dozen, didn't always pay well. With his connections he could find her one of those gems of a job that didn't get advertised in any of the job search websites. Plus, if she handled this right, going to Spain could be the end of her association with him. She wouldn't have to come home and pretend they hadn't kissed—albeit for the benefit of his family. She would be gone. Off to start a new job. A new life. The life she wanted.

"You have lots of friends and connections. I'd need to get a job that would pay me more than this salary. And the job would have to lead to promotions."

"You don't like your job here?"

"I didn't say that."

"I could raise your salary."

"Mitch, if you want me to do this, *today* has to be my last day with Ochoa Online."

He didn't even blink. "Okay."

# CHAPTER TWO

LILA WALKED OUT of the office building that housed Ochoa Online and toward Mitch's black limo, which awaited her on the busy New York City street.

Opening the back door, his driver, Pete, said, "Good morning, Lila."

"Morning, Pete. We'll be stopping two blocks up on the right to pick up my friend Sally."

"Very good."

She slid onto the seat. He closed the door, and she made herself comfortable as he took his position behind the wheel and eased into traffic. Two blocks up, he stopped, jumped out and opened the door for Sally.

When Pete pulled out into traffic again, pretty blonde Sally turned to Lila and said, "All right. Spill. What did you agree to?"

She sucked in a breath. "Two weeks of pretending to be my boss's fiancée. In return, he's going to find me a new job and I'm going to use the extra money I earn to find my mom."

The expression on Sally's face showed that she was trying to understand, but in the end she shook her head. "You are certifiable. Your motives are good, but pretending to be the fiancée of a man you actually like? That's nothing but trouble."

"That's why I couldn't just have him hire a PI to find my mom. Because then I'd still be working for him. I had to ask for a new job so that no matter what happens in Spain it wouldn't follow me home. Once I leave Spain, I'll never see him again. Plus, he assured me that most of the time I'd be on my own while he and his brother, father, uncle and cousin talked business."

"On your own?"

"After I agreed to do this, he told me that I'd spend most of the two weeks with his nanna shopping or running errands, or helping his mom organize the house for a ball a few days after we get there that opens two weeks of celebrations, a second ball the following week to greet latecomers, a reception the night before his brother's wedding and a party the day after."

"You are going to have to be one hell of an actress."

"Or I can just look at it as an extension of my job. I plan Mitch's yearly Christmas party. I plan the business dinners he hosts at his penthouse." She shrugged. "I'm just going to look at it like another Ochoa party."

Sally sighed. "And the other?"

"What other?"

"When you have to be his date?"

"I'll be fine."

"You'll be pee-your-pants nervous."

Lila laughed. "Maybe at first. But I've also decided to look at *that* as an extension of my job."

"Kissing your boss?"

"I'll pigeonhole it somehow."

"You're crazy."

"No. I'm getting a new job out of it. A new *life*." She angled her thumb to point behind them. "Me walking out of that office building a few minutes ago was me walking out forever. I told him the two weeks we spend in Spain are my two-week notice and when we get back I will expect him to have gotten me a new job, one that pays more than what I make with him."

"Wow. You're really leaving."

"I have to. He was surprised when I said I wanted a new job, but when I pushed he didn't seem at all upset to see me go." And that had hurt more than she cared to think about. But it also proved he absolutely had no feelings for her. "He might as well have come right out and said that he desperately needed this favor, or that he just doesn't give a damn that I want another job. Either way, it sort of proves doing this was the right thing. If he needs a fiancée this badly, I have to help him. And if he doesn't care that I want a new job, then it really is time for me to go. It's win/win."

"Are you sure you're not going to be sorry?"

"I've had a crush on this man since the day I met him. He's never noticed me. Only an idiot hangs around forever."

"True."

"And this way I don't merely have a new job that pays enough that I can find my mom." She waved two credit cards. "I get a new wardrobe out of it."

Sally grabbed the cards. "Seriously?"

"Yep. That's why I need your help this morning. I have a hundred-thousand-dollar credit limit on each. Riccardo said use it all. Get everything, including fancy luggage. He said the wedding is formal and I'll also need a gown for the reception the night before. Not to mention the opening ball and a few cocktail parties. He said I'll need enough jeans and shorts and dresses and bathing suits never to be seen in the same thing twice."

Sally gaped at her. "You have hit the jackpot."

"Nope. Believe it or not, Riccardo and Mitch see this as absolutely necessary. I have to look like somebody Mitch would want to marry. To them it's like wardrobe for a play. So, all I have to do is endure two weeks of pretending to be in love with the man I actually do love, and I'll walk away with my freedom, a new job that hopefully pays enough that I can find my mom and enough clothes to be a whole new person."

She also had to not take any of it seriously, keep her wits about her and not end up with a broken heart.

But she didn't tell Sally that. She'd had enough trouble convincing herself she could do it. Sally would never let her go if she thought there was even an inkling of a doubt—and she desperately wanted to find her mom. She wanted the life they'd missed out on.

Oddly, pretending to be in love with the man she actually loved was her ticket away from him and to that life.

Mitch paced the tarmac at ten o'clock the next morning, nervous about this plan. Yesterday, it had seemed like a good idea. Today, thinking about Lila's unruly hair, glasses and frumpy clothes, he found it hard to believe he actually thought they could pull this off. He liked her as an assistant— No. He *loved* her as an assistant. She was smart and thorough and always at his side, ready to do whatever needed to be done. But in the entire time they'd worked together they'd never even had a good enough conversation to tip over into becoming friends.

How in the hell could he have been so desperate to imagine they could pretend to be lovers for two weeks?

His limo suddenly appeared around the corner of the hangar. He'd bought a cab to the airport, leaving Pete and the limo for Lila to make sure she got to the correct place. Seeing them pull up, though, only added to his apprehension. How was he going to pretend to love somebody he barely knew?

The limo stopped. Pete jumped out and opened the back door. One pale pink strappy sandal appeared, then a long length of leg, then the pink hem of a skirt, then Lila stepped out completely. Chestnut-brown hair had been thinned into a sleek, shoulder-length hairdo and now had blond highlights. Her lips were painted a shimmery pink. The little pink dress hugged her curves.

Holy hell.

Big black sunglasses covering half her face, she strolled up to him, a smile curving a lush mouth that he'd never noticed before.

"Do I pass?"

He fought the urge to stutter. "You look—" Unbelievable. Amazing. So different that his tongue stuck to the roof of his mouth. "Very good. Perfect."

"I took you for the sunglasses and miniskirt type."

*And who knew her legs were so long, so shapely?*

He covered his shock at her perception of his taste in women with a nervous laugh. "You maxed out Riccardo's credit cards, didn't you?"

She glanced back at Pete, who pulled suitcase after suitcase out of the car. "He told me to, but I didn't. You don't grow up a foster child without getting some mad skills with money. It would have killed me to pay full price for some of these things. Besides, clearance racks sometimes have the best clothes."

She made a little motion with her fingers for Pete to bring her luggage to the plane, then she headed for the steps. Mitch watched her walk up the short stack and duck into the fuselage, vaguely aware when Pete walked up beside him.

"Who knew, huh?"

"Yeah." Mitch didn't have to ask what Pete was talking about. His Plain Jane assistant looked like she'd stepped off the cover of a magazine. Her high-heeled sandals added a sway to her hips. Sunglasses made her look like someone who summered in the Mediterranean.

Pete said, "Better get going."

Realizing he was standing there gaping like an idiot, he walked to the steps and climbed into the plane. Lila sat on one of the four plush, white leather seats that swiveled and looked like recliners. He stopped.

She peered up at him over her sunglasses. "The pilot told me to sit anywhere and buckle in."

"Pedro?" *The good-looking one?* Why did that make his chest feel like a rock?

She shrugged and pulled an e-reader out of her oversize purse. "I don't know. The guy with the great smile."

It was Pedro. He might not be a millionaire businessman who came from a family with a vineyard, but pilots made a tidy sum, especially private pilots. And the man was a flirt.

He told himself he only cared because Lila was supposed to be his fiancée, and she couldn't use this trip to cruise for dates. "When we get to Spain, you can't be noticing the great smiles of other men."

She laughed. "Jealous?"

"No." The rock from his chest fell to his stomach. He wasn't jealous. This was a make-believe situation. Great hair, sexy body, flirty sunglasses or not, this was still Lila. "I'm saving myself a ton of grief with this ruse. Not to mention that I'm getting the focus off me and onto the happy couple where it belongs. I do not want to spoil my brother's wedding."

He sat on the seat across the aisle and buckled in. Pulling a sheet of paper from the breast pocket of his suit jacket, he swiveled his chair to face her and said, "Riccardo came up with this last night."

She glanced around as if confused. "Where is Riccardo?"

"He took a commercial flight so he could get there ahead of us to pave the way for our story. He's going to tell everyone I'm engaged. He's going to pretend to have let it slip and tell my mom and Nanna they have to behave as if they don't know because I wanted to surprise them."

She frowned. "That's weird."

"No. It adds authenticity to the story. Makes it more believable."

"Ah."

That one syllable gave him a funny feeling that tightened his shoulders and made his eyes narrow. "What's that supposed to mean?"

She laughed. "It just meant I understood." She laughed again. "You're cranky in real life."

"Yeah, well, you're..." She was a knockout in real life. How had he not noticed this? He couldn't remember a damned thing she'd worn to work, which meant it had to be nondescript—nothing worth remembering. Her hair had always been in those odd chopstick things. And her glasses? Thick as Coke bottles.

"You're different too." He finished his thought with a bunch of lame words that didn't come out as much of a comeback.

And that was another thing. When had she gotten so sassy?

He opened the folded sheet of paper. "Riccardo decided that we should stick with the fact that you're my assistant." He glanced up and saw her watching him intently, clearly wanting to get her part down so she could play it. He relaxed a bit, though it did send an unexpected zing through him that she'd taken off the sunglasses. She must be wearing contacts on her smoke-gray eyes. Very sexy smoke-gray eyes that tilted up at the corners and gave her an exotic look.

He cleared his throat. "Anyway, the whole thing started with a long chat one night when we were working late."

She caught his gaze. "We never chatted."

"Yeah, I know." And he suddenly felt sorry

that they hadn't. "But this is make-believe, remember?"

She smiled slightly and nodded.

He sucked in a breath, not liking the nervousness that had invaded him. If he couldn't even read the facts off a sheet, how was he going to perpetuate this charade?

"After our long talk, we started eating dinners together on the nights we were working late."

"Hey, we did do that!"

"But we talked about work."

She bobbed her head. "Yeah, but because we actually did eat dinners together we have another bit of authenticity."

Her answer softened some of the stiffness in his shoulders. "*Sí*. Good." He pulled in a breath and read a little more of Riccardo's story. "Then we started going out to dinner."

She leaned her elbow on the armrest. "We certainly took our time."

He looked up, met the gaze of her soft gray kitten eyes. "I think Riccardo is trying to show we didn't act impulsively."

"God forbid."

He wasn't sure why, but that made him laugh. "Stop. Riccardo's already telling this story and we have to stick to it."

"What if we came up with a totally different set of circumstances? What if we said that one day you ravaged me at work, and we started a passionate affair but we changed the story for Riccardo because we didn't want him to know we couldn't keep our hands off each other?"

All the blood in his veins caught fire. He could picture it. If she'd come to work looking like this he might have ravaged her.

He pulled his collar away from his throat. The plane's engines whined to life.

"Let's just stick with Riccardo's story."

Lila nodded quickly, wishing she hadn't said anything about the passionate affair because with the way he'd been looking at her since she arrived, she could imagine it. If he'd ever, even once, looked at her like that, she might not have been able to resist the temptation to flirt with him—

She'd been flirting with him since he got on the plane. And that was wrong. Wrong. Wrong. Wrong. She didn't want to like him any more than she already did. Worse, she didn't want to become another one of his one-night stands. And that was the real danger in this. That they'd take this charade to the next level, with him thinking it was just a part of the game, and her heart toppling over the edge into something that would only hurt her.

So, no more flirting. She was smarter than this.

She drew in a cleansing breath, gave him what she hoped was a neutral smile and motioned for him to continue. "Go on."

"Riccardo says our dating life was fairly normal. Shows, dinners, weekends in Vegas and the Hamptons."

She nodded, liking the dispassionate direction the conversation had taken. "Your family's house in the Hamptons is pretty." When he gave her a puzzled look, she added, "Riccardo showed me pictures."

"He goes there more than I do. But it's good you

know what the place looks like. That'll probably come in handy."

He sounded so nervous that she smiled again. "You don't like this charade."

"I don't like lying to my family. But this is necessary. It isn't just the fact that I don't want to be hounded by Nanna. This is Alonzo and Julia's big celebration. The focus shouldn't be on me. Not in any way, shape or form."

"You don't think your engagement will be reason for them to make you the center of attention?"

"We'll let them fawn one night. Tonight. Then after that when they get too happy or too focused on us, we remind them that it's Julia and Alonzo's celebration. Not ours."

"Makes sense." She cocked her head. "You really are over her."

He sighed. "I've said it a million times. No one seems to believe me."

"Maybe because everybody knows getting over your brother's betrayal would be harder."

He sniffed a laugh. "When'd you get so perceptive?"

"I've always been perceptive. That's how I stay one step ahead of what you need."

He nodded, as if just figuring that out, and sadness started in her stomach and expanded into her chest. He might think her pretty in the pink dress, showing off her legs and even being a little sassy with him, but in the end she was still the assistant he barely noticed.

But that was good. If she was going to start a new life when they returned, she didn't want to do it with a broken heart. A woman who needed to find her mom and fix their damaged past couldn't afford to make stupid mistakes. Though she'd always believed she was destined for something great, she also realized that that fairy tale had just been a vehicle to keep her sane, keep her working toward things like her high school diploma and eventually a degree. Lately the desire for "something great" was taking a back seat to the things she really wanted: her mom. A family. That's why her crush on Mitch had seemed so pointless that she'd decided it was time to move on.

Mitch's groan of disgust brought her out of her

reverie. "That's the stupidest engagement story I've ever heard."

Oh, crap. He'd been reading Riccardo's notes and she'd missed something important. "Read it again. Let me think it through."

He gaped at her. "How would you possibly need to hear it again? It's ridiculous. I wouldn't rent a hot air balloon. I wouldn't hire a skywriter to spell out the proposal at sunset so I could get down on one knee in a balloon."

She laughed. Wow. That was bad. "Okay. So it's a bit schmaltzy."

"It's pedestrian."

"What would you have done in real life?"

He sighed. "What I'd planned for Julia was to come home early, pour two flutes of champagne, walk around the apartment until I found her, tell her she was beautiful and I wanted her in my life forever...then give her the ring."

"Oh." Her breath wobbled. His proposal idea was perfect. Elegant in its simplicity. "That would have been nice."

"Yeah, if I hadn't caught her with my brother."

She laughed, then stopped herself. How was it that he could make her laugh over something that had probably broken his heart—even though he seemed to be over it?

"Well, it was a great proposal idea."

"I thought so too. But apparently my brother did some grand gesture on the yacht."

"Oh, I get what Riccardo's doing. He's making sure our proposal keeps up with Alonzo and Julia's. But maybe he's making things suspicious by thinking you need to compete with Alonzo."

"I'm not like my brother."

"Plus, simple is better sometimes."

He met her gaze. "Exactly. He should have said something more me. Like I gave you the ring, then stripped you naked and we spent the weekend in bed."

This time her breath froze. If Riccardo had come up with that scenario for their engagement story, she wouldn't be able to breathe anytime anyone told it. Better to stick with the fake one.

"So maybe the hot air balloon idea is a good one."

"It's not me."

"We'll try not to tell it too often. We'll use the 'this is Julia and Alonzo's celebration' excuse."

He nodded. "Good idea."

He focused his attention on the sheet of facts Riccardo had written up, but stopped reading out loud. Her gaze swept the five o'clock shadow growing on his chin and cheeks, then rose to his nearly black eyes and up to his shiny black hair. Her fingers itched to run through the thick locks, and it suddenly struck her that maybe sometime in the next two weeks she could.

Just as her heart stumbled in her chest, his gaze rose and he smiled at her. "Riccardo also says this flight would be a good time for us to exchange stories."

"Exchange stories?"

"He thinks I should tell you about things like the time I jumped off the roof of one of the winery's outbuildings, thinking I could fly."

She didn't know whether to laugh or gape at him. "Why would you think you could fly?"

"I was eight and I had a cape."

A laugh burst from her. "That's hysterical."

"Didn't you ever do anything stupid?"

Her earliest memories were of her mom sleeping on the couch. She'd sit on the floor in front of the sofa and watch her mother's chest rise and fall, being scared silly because technically she was alone. Four years old and all alone. She was six or seven before she realized her mom kept sleeping because she drank too much alcohol. And it wasn't until she was ten that she understood what a hangover was.

The only stupid thing she'd done was mention that to a social worker.

# CHAPTER THREE

"I LED A very quiet life."

Even as that statement came out of Lila's mouth, Mitch remembered her answer when he'd asked if she'd maxed out the company credit cards Riccardo had given her. "Weren't you a foster child?"

She brushed at her dress, as if trying to smooth out nonexistent wrinkles. "Yes. But that doesn't mean my life was exciting."

He knew little about the American foster care system, but he did understand the basics. A child was taken in by a family who was paid by the state to care for him or her. He supposed that left little room for being silly or stupid or even experimental, if you wanted to keep your home. Because if you didn't keep your home—

The picture that brought to mind tightened his chest. Not wanting to think of Lila as a child on the street, alone and scared, and not wanting to examine his motives for the emptiness that invaded his soul just considering that she might have been alone or scared, he changed the subject.

"How were your grades?"

She grinned. "I was a star."

He knew that, of course. They'd checked into her when they'd hired her. She'd been top of her class everywhere from elementary school to university.

"Anything I should know about your love life?"

She glanced across the aisle at him, caught his gaze. "No."

"At least tell me the story of your first date."

She smoothed her hair off her forehead. "Oh. Well, I guess that depends on what you consider a date. I had a huge crush on my next-door neighbor when I was five."

He laughed. "Not that far back."

"Okay. I went to the prom in high school."

"Seriously? That was your first date?"

She shrugged. "I was busy getting those good grades, remember?"

He sighed. "All right. If we really were engaged, I probably wouldn't know every corner of your love life. But give me something I can take to Nanna that will convince her we're…" He paused, grappling for words, because now that he was getting to know her everything felt funny. He'd already pictured himself ravaging her. Her fault. She'd brought it up. But, because he'd already seen it in his head, he couldn't quite say *lovers* out loud.

Finally he just sucked it up and said, "To help her believe we're intimate."

"Oh, my gosh. Seriously? Did you just say that? You couldn't say lovers…or that we're having sex or even knocking boots?" She laughed heartily. "Mitch, you have got to lighten up. You'll do more to convince your grandmother we're engaged with your actions than you will remembering a bunch of useless information about my life."

Irritated with himself for all these weird reactions, he said, "Yeah, I guess."

She caught his gaze again. But this time the

light of humor brightened her pretty eyes. "I *know*."

The awkwardness of being so informal with her pressed in on him again, and he had to get rid of it. Since she seemed to like humor so much, he went in that direction and said, "I suppose this means you're not going to tell me the story of how you lost your virginity."

She laughed. "No. And I don't want to hear about yours."

"Mine's a great story," he teased, so relieved that the tension had been broken that he decided to keep her laughing.

"I'll bet."

"I was about fifteen. A middle-aged woman came to the winery for a tour—"

"Oh, my God!" She put her hands over her ears. "Stop."

"All right. I suppose that one isn't exactly G-rated. Want to hear about Riccardo's?"

Her eyes widened comically.

But he realized something important. "If we really were engaged, you might not know about our sex lives, but you would know about Riccardo's and my antics as kids. So what do you say I tell you some of those stories?"

She slowly pulled her hands away from her ears. "Okay. If I were your fiancée for real, I would know those."

"Exactly."

He told her about skipping school, climbing trees, swimming in the lake behind his family's property before the family put in the in-ground pool. He told her about Nanna covering for him and Riccardo a time or two, then using her knowledge for blackmail.

"Your nanna's a pistol."

"You don't know the half of it."

"Thus the reason for the fake fiancée."

"*Sí.*" He paused a second, then said, "So what about you?"

She smiled at him from across the aisle. "What about me?"

"What do I need to know about you to fool my grandmother?"

"Nothing."

"Oh, come on, I have to tell her something."

"Nope. I'm a nonentity in this charade. I don't matter. Just as Riccardo made up stories about our getting together and your proposal, I can be anything you need me to be because two weeks from now I'm out of the picture."

"But doesn't it make more sense to use your real life?" He peeked at her. "You know...for authenticity."

"Then we'd trip over into too many details that wouldn't fit. Since we didn't actually start dating." Her eyes met his. "We never even became friends. It's easier for us to make up a background that's more suited to a woman you'd date."

Though what she'd said made sense, irritation slid through him. Why was she arguing? Evading him?

"That's just the point. For better or worse you *are* the woman I chose. So I think it would make more sense if we figured out *why* I chose you— sticking with the truth—rather than to make up a story that we'd have to remember. Riccardo's story is that we started talking and became friends." He smiled his most charming smile. "So let's become friends."

She just looked at him. Her pretty gray eyes softened with a sort of sadness. He expected her to argue again, but she said, "I live in a walk-up in Brooklyn. I put myself through university as a barista in a coffee place. I sort of live to work." She opened her hands. "Honestly, no hobbies. Nothing really interesting about me."

"You have to have more to your life than that."

She shook her head. "Unless you want to dip into the foster child stuff—which I don't—I am as dull as watching paint dry."

He would have accepted that, except she avoided his eyes and looked away quickly, the way a person does when they are lying or hiding something.

She did live in a walk-up in Brooklyn.

She had put herself through university as a barista.

She'd told him both of those in her employment interview. So if she wasn't lying she was hiding something.

He knew it for certain when she firmly said, "Okay. Once we get over the initial introductions, I'll just keep deflecting questions by reminding everybody this is Alonzo and Julia's weekend. There's no reason to get fancy about this."

He nodded, but his gut knotted. Why would she want to keep something from him? *What* would she want to keep from him? It couldn't be a criminal record—her record had been clean when he hired her. Which meant she didn't sell drugs. Or rob banks. Or even have a permit to carry a gun. But maybe she dated losers? Or collected spiders? Or was one of those people who dressed up like a zombie and went to those weird parties—

Maybe he didn't want to know?

After all, as she'd said, this charade would be over in two weeks. And if he forced the issue, he'd know an ugly detail of her life that he probably shouldn't know.

When five minutes went by with neither of them saying anything, she pulled out her e-reader.

Trepidation filled him again. She was about to walk into the heart of his family. They would ask her a million questions. Yes, he understood that she could make up answers about their dating and her life, since this whole deal was fake, but—

No buts. She was right. They'd spent a year working together, not getting to know each other. If she had a private life she wanted to keep private, he should just accept that and trust that she could handle this ruse.

He relaxed a bit, settled back in his seat, used the remote to activate the television and nodded off thinking that his assistant had handled every job he'd ever given her. He should trust that whatever she wasn't telling him it wasn't relevant to her job—

Except she wanted to leave his employ and she'd never fully explained why.

Damn it! What the hell was up with her?

The jet landed in Spain a little after one o'clock in the morning, Spain time. The pilot's announcement woke Lila and she yawned and stretched.

"So much for meeting your family tonight."

Mitch blew his breath out on a groan that spoke

of someone desperately wanting to continue sleeping. "I don't know how I got so scattered that I forgot about the time difference, but we'll get to the winery by two. I can show you to your room and you can either go back to sleep or take a shower or something to wake yourself up enough you can adjust to the new time zone."

She waved her e-reader at him. "Don't worry about me. I can always entertain myself."

He smiled tiredly. "Great."

His unenthusiastic tone sent a little jangle skipping along Lila's nerve endings. Now that they were on the ground in Spain, near his family, he didn't seem as convinced about this plan as he had in New York City. And part of that might be her fault. He hadn't been pleased that she refused to talk about her past. But, really, they'd spent a year together and he'd never once asked her what she'd done over the weekend, let alone chitchatted about her past. So maybe a little part of her had decided to hold back. But she was still right about the ruse. It would be too difficult to explain how a high-powered executive, a charmer with a killer smile and tons of money, would want *her*. He hadn't wanted *her* in a whole year. They were better off to make up an interesting past for her that turned her into a woman who would attract him and keep his interest enough that he'd want to marry her.

They exited the plane and Lila stood by Mitch as they waited for the copilot and limo driver to unload their luggage and pile it into the trunk of a big black car.

Finally finished, the driver opened the back door of the vehicle and greeted Mitch. *"Buenas noches."*

Mitch laughed. "Shouldn't that be *buenos días*?"

The driver chuckled. *"Sí."*

*Good day rather than good night.*

Lila had to agree with that because it was after midnight, already an hour into the new day, except her body was on New York time. Though she'd had a nap on the plane, a few hours from now when his family was waking, she'd want to go to sleep for real.

Once they were settled on the long, comfortable

back seat, Mitch said, "Don't worry. My family and the entire staff speak English."

She shrugged. "I toyed around with being a social worker, so I took enough Spanish in college that I'm fluent."

He frowned. "You thought about being a social worker?"

"Everybody does." She met his gaze, throwing him a bone with a little personal information since she'd clearly insulted him before when she wouldn't tell him anything beyond the basics. "Everybody wants to save the world."

Shaking his head, he said, "Not my family." He motioned toward the window even though she could see nothing in the dead of night through the darkened glass. "We have a legacy to protect."

"I think that's kinda nice. You know—" She lifted one shoulder slightly, trying to be nonchalant, even though she envied him and his casual acceptance of not just having a mom and dad, a brother, a nanna, an aunt and uncle and a cousin, but also a legacy. "A place to belong."

"Oh, we belong all right. Sometimes I feel like an indentured servant."

She studied him, confused that he couldn't see how lucky he was. "Is that why you came to New York?"

"My father released me to more or less follow my dream of setting up a website to sell Ochoa wines online after I caught Alonzo and Julia together. There was no way Dad could have picked sides. Picked one son over the other. Especially since what I'd walked in on was basically Alonzo and Julia's first kiss. I'd more or less been ignoring her, traveling around Europe, trying to sell wine. So I didn't have to do a lot of soul-searching to realize I didn't really love her, and from the way Alonzo protected Julia the next few days, it was clear he did. Allowing me to create and head up Ochoa Online and move it anywhere I wanted, my dad put a positive spin on what could have potentially caused a huge rift in our family."

"And then you came to New York and you were successful and now it all seems to have had a purpose."

He tilted his head. "That's basically how it's panned out. Except I took it one step further, started the general wine site and headed off in my own direction. Forged my own success. I don't want this wedding to take the luster off the fact that I stepped away and started my own businesses, any more than I want to have people thinking of me instead of my brother during what should be the happiest time of Alonzo's life."

She nodded, totally understanding. But she didn't want to know too much more or to tell him too much more about herself. That would be a heck of a lot like confiding, a heck of a lot like actually becoming friends, and that was risky to her heart. Not to mention the fact that he might not think highly of a little girl who'd gotten herself sent into foster care and cost her mom a chance to pull herself together and become a good parent.

Worse, while he had told her the stories about himself and Riccardo, she'd pictured him as a devilish little boy and her heartstrings had tugged. So no more confiding. She had to stay strong.

"Oh, I almost forgot." He reached into his jacket pocket and pulled out a small black velvet ring box.

Her gaze leaped to his.

He smiled as he opened it. "Will you marry me?"

He said it casually, but her breath froze in wonderment. She remembered her first day of working with him, how he'd knocked her for a loop with his good looks and charm, remembered how much she loved that he was strong and smart. She thought of all the things that she imagined she would think about if he were asking her to marry him for real. Her heart lodged in her throat and her chest got so tight she could barely breathe, but she reminded herself this wasn't real. And that falling into this kind of emotional land mine was the very thing she had to avoid.

So she laughed and said, "Sure," as if her feelings weren't going in a million directions, and she was able to see the humor in their charade.

He slid the rock on her third finger, left hand, and instantly her hand sank along with her heart.

Not only was it the biggest diamond she'd ever seen, but it was the most beautiful ring ever crafted, and it was all a sham.

Determined not to fall into any more emotional traps, she glanced up at him with a smile. "Wow. I hope you didn't pay for this by the ounce."

He laughed. "It's on consignment."

The reminder that for him this was temporary, just a means to an end, a way to accomplish a goal for his family and himself, fortified her. Especially since she was being rewarded for her part. If she wanted a new job, money to hire a PI to find her mom and ultimately a new life, there could be no more slipups. She had to make this look real. And she could do it. It wasn't like she hadn't faked her way through things before. As a child she'd had to pretend to like potatoes or peas or ham so her new foster mom wouldn't think her too picky, and plenty of times she'd had to pretend to love certain television shows just to fit in. When she left that life, she'd vowed she'd be herself for the rest of her days and never pretend again, but this was for a good cause. Two good causes. Mitch could keep the focus of this wedding on his brother and she would find her mom.

Faking to make it work made perfect sense.

They traveled through a country she couldn't see for forty minutes, then the limo stopped. When the driver opened the door, she saw the magnificent stone mansion in front of her. Two stories and clearly built centuries ago, the house stood like a sentinel, taking care of its occupants, marking the passage of time with lines and wrinkles pressed into the stone by wind and rain.

As she stepped out of the limo, she said, "It's fantastic."

The air felt different. Or maybe the knowledge that she was on a different continent had her sensing that the warm air around them was sweeter, earthier.

"The upstairs contains Nanna and my parents' residences. Winery is in the basement beside a restaurant. First floor holds business offices, tour information and gift shop."

*Well, there went all the romance out of that.*

"Oh."

"Don't pout." He put his hands on her shoulders and turned her to the right. "We have an apartment in the second building down."

His voice had dipped low, as if he really was talking to a girlfriend. The place where his hands rested on her shoulders felt like it was on fire. A shower of tingles rained down her spine.

More nervous than she'd ever imagined she could be, she turned, hoping to get out from under his warm fingers. "And the first building is?"

"Alonzo and Julia's home. He runs the winery. It's only fitting he has a house." He smiled casually. "I'm just a guest now."

*Had she heard a little sadness in that? A dollop of emotion?*

She studied his dark, dark eyes. There was no hurt in the black orbs. No rancor. He did not begrudge his brother his success. But there also didn't seem to be an attachment to this wonderful home—this *legacy*—that she would give half her heart and most of her soul to be a part of.

She broke the connection and turned toward the two newer buildings. Her nerves eased a bit.

The last thing she wanted was to find herself in the same house with his relatives. This way she had private space.

Mitch put his hand on the small of her back and guided her to the second building. In the muted glow of small lamps to light the path, she could see lush green grass that created comfortable lawns, but little else.

Vaguely aware that the driver pulled their things from the back of the limo, she allowed Mitch to lead her up the cobblestone path to a front door and into a quiet foyer with a set of stairs to the second floor. He nodded for her to climb them.

As they walked up the thin stairway, she realized his eyes were about level with her butt. That might have made her nervous, except she remembered the casual way he'd given her the ring and knew she had nothing to worry about. When they reached the second floor, he pulled keys out of his pocket, unlocked the door and gave it a nudge to open it. He granted her entry first, then flipped on a light.

*"Surprise!"*

The room was full of dark-haired, dark-eyed people she assumed were his relatives. Pressing her hand to her chest to stop her galloping heart, she turned to Mitch.

He quickly caught her hand. "Mom, Dad!" he said, glancing around. "Everybody's here."

The woman around fifty, with streaks of white in her shiny black hair, raced over. When she grabbed Mitch's shoulders, went up on tiptoe and hugged him, Lila guessed she was his mother.

"Why didn't you tell us you were engaged?"

He looked around as if totally perplexed, but Lila caught his ploy. Apparently, Riccardo had done his part and "slipped" the engagement to his family and they'd planned this gathering. Mitch was reacting the way he would if he really were engaged. "I wanted to tell you in person."

Riccardo stepped forward. "Sorry, cuz. I accidentally let the cat out of the bag."

Everyone laughed, and Lila watched them in amazement. Riccardo had been correct. Pretending to let it slip that Mitch was engaged had actually made it all seem real. But, oh my goodness, he had so much family. And all of them close enough to welcome him home.

Mitch dropped her hand but slid his arm around her shoulders and nestled her against his side. "Everyone, this is my fiancée, Lila."

Mitch's mom hugged her fiercely, then burst into tears. "Both of my boys are gone now."

Mitch chuckled. "Not gone, Mom. Just getting married."

Everyone laughed. Someone in the back said, "They should make it a double wedding."

Lila held back a gasp of horror, but Mitch said, "Not on your life. We want our own celebration and think Alonzo and Julia are entitled to theirs."

A man who looked like Mitch held his glass high. "Hear! Hear!"

Mitch turned to her and said, "Lila, that is my brother, Alonzo."

She smiled. "Nice to meet you."

Mitch quickly ran through the introductions, starting with the closest person, his mom, Marguerite, then on to his dad, his aunt and uncle, Julia and Alonzo, and finally a small gray-haired woman in the back.

"Nanna."

She eased through the small jumble of people. "So, you stole my grandson's heart."

She glanced up at Mitch. Something inside her wouldn't let her lie, so she laughed and said, "He certainly stole mine."

Mitch's dad, Santiago, the tall, dark-haired man with white hair at his temples, pulled a bottle of wine from a small wooden washtub filled with ice and many other bottles of wine. "Get me two glasses so we can toast."

Riccardo immediately produced two beautiful, intricately patterned wineglasses. Santiago took them and began to fill them.

"Oh, no need to fill a second glass," Lila quickly said, before he poured. "I'll just have some orange juice for the toast. I don't drink."

A weird hush fell over the room. Foreheads wrinkled in confusion. All eyes jumped to her.

Nanna said, "You don't drink?"

"No. But I'd love to toast with a glass of orange juice or even water."

"You're dating a man whose family owns a winery…but you don't drink?"

"Forget about that," Santiago said with a laugh. "You *work* for a winery. You did meet because you're his assistant, correct? That means you work for a winery."

Marguerite said, "How can you take a job with a winery when you don't drink?"

*Because she took one look at Marguerite's son and couldn't say no?*

"I'm not opposed to other people drinking."

Mitch stole a peek at Lila, his head spinning. How could he have missed that she didn't drink?

Elegant Marguerite recovered first. "Riccardo, a glass of orange juice, please."

Obviously his family had stocked his apartment in anticipation of his arrival because Riccardo went to the kitchen and returned with a pitcher of orange juice. He poured a glass and handed it to Mitch's dad, who also held a glass of wine for Mitch.

Santiago gave the drinks to Mitch and Lila. She

took hers with a smile and he inwardly sighed with relief.

"To my son and his fiancée." Santiago's eyes crinkled at the corners when he grinned. "I expect a wedding this time next year." Everyone laughed. "Our family is truly blessed. *Salud.*"

"*Salud!*"

Everyone took a sip of their wine. Lila downed her entire glass of orange juice as if she was either dying of thirst or so nervous she couldn't stop herself.

"Thank you, everyone, for the toast and for meeting us." He glanced at Lila again. She didn't appear to be falling apart, but after her gulping down the juice he didn't want to risk it. He didn't want her saying something from which they couldn't recover. He wasn't entirely sure they'd recovered from the fact that she didn't drink. "But we're exhausted. Can we finish this celebration in the morning?"

Nanna said, "Of course! We will make the best breakfast ever cooked."

Mitch shook his head. "No! This is Alonzo and

Julia's celebration. Not ours. We'll be back in the fall and you can celebrate properly if you wish."

His mom nodded. "Yes. You are correct. This is Alonzo and Julia's time. Now that we have toasted your engagement, we can go back to celebrating the wedding."

The family began to file out. Each stopped and took the chance to shake his hand and hug Lila, who hung in there like a trooper.

Finally Nanna stepped up. She hugged Lila, saying, "Welcome to the family." Then hugged Mitch. He could feel the tension of the first meeting ebbing away as she pulled out of the embrace.

Then she looked him in the eye and said, "While Lila gets settled, why don't you and I take a minute to catch up, *Nene*?"

His heart sank. To the casual observer, her request was the simple longing of a grandmother to spend time with her grandson. But she'd called him baby boy, the term she'd always used right before she scolded him.

"Of course."

She turned and started to the door, but stopped

suddenly and faced him, motioning with her fingers for him to follow her. She wanted him to leave with her. There'd be no reprieve. No couple of minutes to pull himself together. He had to go now.

He glanced at Lila. "I won't be long."

Her smoky gray eyes clouded with fear. "I'll be fine."

The look in her silvery orbs didn't match her words. She sounded relieved. She looked totally shell-shocked.

"Oh, come on already," Nanna said with a sigh. "I'm an old woman, getting older, and I need my sleep. Kiss her goodbye so we can get going."

His heart chugged to a stop and he understood how Lila could sound relieved and look terrified. Nothing had gone as they'd planned. Once they'd landed and he remembered the time difference, he'd believed they'd sneak in under the cover of darkness, get a little sleep, then go to an ordinary breakfast in a few hours, be bombarded by well-wishers and sit down and eat eggs. Instead, they walked into a group of his family lying in wait. And now he had to kiss her.

Obviously, she didn't want him to.

His male pride took a direct hit. It wasn't like he was Frankenstein. Hell, most women considered him good-looking. Yet, this woman he'd seen almost every day for a year seemed appalled at the thought of kissing him.

Putting his hands on her shoulders, he brushed his lips across hers quickly, not even pausing when a little zap of something set his hormones humming and sent an unexpected urge to linger through him. She was Lila, for heaven's sake.

He pulled away, a bit surprised by the stunned expression on her face. It matched the weird jumpy feeling he had in his stomach. His hands slid from her shoulders, down her arms to her hands, and for a few seconds he didn't want to let go. He liked the feeling of her small, soft hands in his. He wanted to investigate the weird buzz of confusion.

But Nanna cleared her throat.

He followed her out of the apartment, closing the door behind him, still feeling a little shaky from the odd reaction to a kiss that was nothing more than a touch. When Nanna didn't talk on the way to the main house, through the high-ceilinged foyer, up the stairs and into the living room of her quarters, he was glad. He wasn't sure he could have spoken without his confusion coming through.

Nanna perched on a Queen Anne chair as if it was a throne and, out of habit, he walked behind the shiny mahogany bar and poured her a small glass of red.

After handing it to her, he sat down. Trepidation raced through him. In all the confusion of that kiss, he'd forgotten Nanna wanted to interrogate him.

Damn it! He shouldn't have let Lila get away with evading his questions about her past because now he had virtually nothing to tell Nanna.

"So, your fiancée, she is pregnant?"

Mitch's heart slammed to a halt, as his eyes bulged. "What? No!"

"The baby's not yours, then?"

*"What?"*

"Why else does she not drink?"

"There are a million reasons a person doesn't drink." And right now he wished to hell he'd asked her. Damn it. How could a woman who doesn't drink work for a winery—

He paused his thoughts. That was actually a very telling thing. If she could work for a winery that might mean her reasons for abstaining weren't serious ones. Like, maybe, she didn't like the taste of alcohol? Or maybe she didn't want the extra calories—

"She's so casual about not drinking that I never asked her. At first, I was only her boss. So I figured it was none of my business." He shrugged. "Now? I just assume it has to do with watching her calories. She's crazy about keeping her figure."

There. His ass was totally covered. He'd as much as said he didn't know, yet there were valid reasons for not knowing. He had been lucky this time, but there was no guarantee he'd be lucky the next. When he got back to his apartment they were going to have to have a long talk.

"So she's not pregnant?"

"No."

Nanna set her wineglass down and laid her hands on her lap demurely. "Hmm…"

"No 'hmm,' Nanna. She's not pregnant." And even if she was, they'd be gone in two weeks, the fake engagement over, and no one in this family needed to know. Except—

What if she was pregnant? What if that was why she needed a job that paid her more?

"It's just that she has a certain glow. A happiness that women get when they are pregnant."

"Did you ever stop to think that maybe she's happy to be engaged to me."

Nanna laughed slightly.

"Now what's *that* supposed to mean?"

She rose. "You are too suspicious."

"Oh, yeah? I'm not the one who jumped to the conclusion that my girlfriend was pregnant."

"Fiancée."

He scrubbed his hand across the back of his neck. Another mistake. He should be smarter than this. On his toes. Especially with the woman he needed to fool. "She's been my girlfriend so long that I sometimes lapse."

"Really? Because according to records she's only been your assistant for a year."

"Right."

"Then you started dating right after she went to work for you?"

"Sort of, but—" He thought of Lila's suggestion that he'd ravaged her in his office one night but they hadn't told Riccardo and smiled. "Actually, Nanna, Riccardo doesn't know everything about our relationship. And it might not be appropriate for you to know either."

She laughed. "Oh, *Nene*. You are truly the bad boy of the family. But this woman, Lila. She is sweet. It will hurt me if you hurt her."

"We're engaged, Nanna. I'm not going to hurt her." The lie stuck in his throat like stale peanut butter. Not just because he didn't like lying but because it never once occurred to him that he could hurt Lila. This was a business deal. She knew that. He knew that. Why was he thinking about stupid things?

Nanna squeezed his hand. "Good night."

He said, "Good night," watching her leave the

living room and head back the hall to her bedroom. When she was gone, he looked skyward and rolled his eyes. He'd certainly accomplished his purpose of taking everybody's mind off his reaction to Julia and Alonzo getting married, but he should have thought twice about where he'd chosen to put their attention.

He headed for his apartment, knocked twice, lightly, because he was an idiot, involved in a scheme with a woman he didn't know, who he was going to have to learn completely before breakfast the next morning, then he opened the door and walked into the empty living room.

"Crap." He hoped to heaven she wasn't in the shower and wondered if he should go looking for her. Because that was another thing he'd forgotten about this charade. She could be stark naked behind either of the bedroom doors.

# CHAPTER FOUR

TWO MINUTES AFTER Mitch left with his nanna, the driver brought their bags to the apartment, immediately turning left and stacking them in the larger of the two bedrooms.

He made three trips and all three times, Lila had smiled and thanked him. But when he left for the final time, she darted into the room with the luggage, grabbed her bags and set herself up in the second bedroom. Mitch was gone so long she'd taken a quick rinse in the shower, put on her pajama pants and a T-shirt and crawled into bed. Just before she would have fallen asleep out of sheer exhaustion, the apartment door opened and quietly closed.

He was back.

Her breath stalled as she waited in silence, wondering if he would realize she was already in bed and simply head for the room where the driver had left his bags. He'd gone to that bedroom without any instruction from her and she'd decided that had to mean it was the room Mitch typically used. She certainly didn't think he expected her to be in his bed.

So, if she was lucky, he'd figure out she was in the other room and let her sleep.

"Lila!"

She squeezed her eyes shut. Nope. Not lucky.

"Lila! We need to talk."

Oh, she didn't think so. Her plan was to play a role so she could keep enough emotional distance between them that she didn't fall any more in love with him than she already was. So talking was absolutely out. Especially since she had the sneaking feeling his nanna might be a little harder to fool than Mitch believed, and that's why his voice sounded so edgy. Sweet little Nanna had wanted to talk to him in private. Of course she had reservations. And Lila didn't want to discuss any of them.

"I refuse to go to breakfast tomorrow with my

family unable to give even simple facts about you. Not to mention the big questions dredged up by your announcement that you don't drink."

This time she winced. It had never even occurred to her that she was a nondrinker working for a winery. For her, work was a way to make a living—and her job had also been about being with him, hoping he would notice her. Ironic that she intended to avoid him as much as she could in their last two weeks together.

A long space of silence ensued. She waited, not breathing, praying he didn't open the door and find her lying in bed with covers up to her chin, hiding her worn pajama pants and New York Giants T-shirt. If he came in now, he'd be talking to the real Lila. Not the fancy girl in the pink dress and tall sandals. That girl could handle him. Real Lila would stutter.

"All right. If you're sleeping, fine."

She pressed her fingers to her lips to stop a laugh. It was just like Mitch to keep talking to someone he thought was sleeping. He never let a thought go unfinished.

Her smile faded. That meant first thing in the morning they'd be having the talk she was avoiding now.

She'd better dress pretty damned dazzling to have enough confidence to keep him at bay the way she had in the airplane.

In spite of her worry, she fell asleep almost immediately. Having set her phone alarm for six o'clock, Spain time, she got up when it sounded and headed for her closet, ready to jump into this problem and solve it. The pink dress had worked to keep him slightly off his game the day before. So she'd have to find something like that. She flicked a few hangers to the left, then realized she shouldn't get too dressed up for a breakfast. She pulled a white lace top out of the closet and matched it with a pair of skinny jeans and flat sandals. Fixing her hair the sleek way she had it the day before, she decided she had the best of both worlds. A sleek, sophisticated hairdo and contact lenses that made her look like a different person, paired with an ordinary outfit that said she was a comfortable, easygoing person, who oozed confidence.

She made a long assessment of herself in the full-length mirror. If she had to say so herself, she'd chosen well. The outfit made her appear casually sexy, as if sexy was her natural state. She looked so unlike herself that she felt like she was seeing a stranger. But that was good. The only way she would manage to keep her distance with Mitch would be to remember this was all playacting, and there was no better way to get yourself into character than with a costume.

Satisfied, she walked out of her bedroom and found Mitch in the sitting area, on the sofa, reading a newspaper, probably a *Wall Street Journal* that he'd brought with him. When she closed the door behind her, the paper rustled as it lowered.

For a few seconds, Mitch said nothing but the expression on his face spoke volumes. His eyebrows rose. His lips twitched, going from a smile to a frown and back up into a smile again.

"Do I pass?"

"Ridiculously. That's one of the reasons I think

we need to talk. I can't quite reconcile you with the Lila who works for me."

"You're not supposed to connect me to who I am for real. I'm a *fake* fiancée, remember?" She motioned around herself. "All this is smoke and mirrors. Something *you need* to take the focus off you and put it on your brother and his bride."

He sucked in a breath. "All right. I get that, but last night Nanna—"

The phone rang. Mitch's face became like a thundercloud at the interruption. He grabbed the receiver. "Yes! What!"

There was a pause, then he jumped from the sofa and squeezed his eyes shut. "Sorry, Nanna!"

Wearing cargo shorts and a golf shirt, the kind he usually wore when they worked Saturdays in the summer, he was 100 percent Mitcham Ochoa. Except that his nanna really seemed to be able to push all his buttons.

"Right. I know we eat promptly at seven, but Lila and I—" He stopped. His face twisted with horror. "There was no hanky-panky, Nanna! We just slept in. We are on our way downstairs now."

He hung up the phone and Lila sucked in a breath. "She's a tough one."

"Which is exactly why we need to talk."

"No," Lila said, racing to the door. "We're late. We need to get down to breakfast and keep the conversation on your brother and Julia."

Mitch followed her. As he closed the apartment door, she ran down the steps, knowing that once they got outside he wouldn't ask questions because they'd be within hearing distance of anybody milling about on the grounds. But success right now only provided a short reprieve. After breakfast, she'd have to give him a darned good reason for not drinking. And it couldn't be foolish. It had to work.

It just couldn't be the real one.

She wanted a clean break when they got home. So he couldn't empathize or sympathize with her. She didn't want any emotion at all between them. Not even friendship. When she walked out of his life in two weeks, she didn't want either one of them looking back.

He caught up to her as she started across the

empty parking lot to the sidewalk that led to the house. He took her hand and she gave him a brief smile, though her heart began to chug and all of a sudden heat infused her. Real Lila couldn't handle things like holding hands, and she realized that though she'd gotten into costume, she kept falling out of character.

She took a second to remind herself she was playing the part of a rich guy's fiancée, and she was in Spain. Gorgeous Spain! Where the sun glistened on the dew coating the leaves in the rows and rows of grapevines. Rolling hills stretched to black mountains. And the sky was such a perfect blue it almost took her breath away.

"It's beautiful here."

"It's summer. Everywhere is beautiful in the summer."

"Yes. I guess." She glanced around at the grounds. Healthy green grass and trees gave way to a plethora of grapevines that seemed to go on forever. "Your family must make a lot of wine."

He laughed. "How else do you think we support three generations of Ochoas?"

"By making a lot of wine."

He shook his head. "By *selling* a lot of wine."

He opened the door for her and she stepped into the lobby of the main house turned business premises. On the right were shelves filled with bottles displaying the Ochoa label, as well as touristy trinkets, T-shirts and corks with the vineyard's logo. On the left was a silent corridor. Mitch had told her the family's business offices were on this level, and she assumed that hall led to those offices.

Remembering the restaurant in the basement, she said, "Do we go downstairs?"

"Upstairs. To the residences."

"Okay."

Once again they climbed a flight of stairs, a circular stairway wide enough for them to walk side by side. A huge sitting room greeted them at the top of the steps with corridors jutting left and right.

"My parents' quarters are that way," Mitch said, pointing to the left. "And Nanna lives down here." He directed her to walk to the right.

At the end of the hall they entered a door that opened onto another sitting room, then Mitch led her to a dining room where it seemed the entire Ochoa family had gathered at a long cherrywood table.

The men rose. Mitch walked Lila to the two empty places at the table, pulled out her chair and helped her sit before he sat beside her.

As the men returned to their seats, Julia said, "Jeans at the breakfast table! Lila, what a bold woman you are!"

A quick glance around showed all the women were dressed up. Though the men were a lot more casual, like Mitch.

"I thought you were coming with us this morning while I pick up my gown for tonight's opening gala?"

Lila smiled at Mitch, then Julia. "Actually, I didn't know that. But I'd love to come." She wasn't sure if Julia was being catty, but she could handle a million Julias. It was a morning alone with Mitch she needed to get out of. "Give me ten minutes after breakfast and I can be ready."

Julia smiled. "So you're a quick-change artist."

That was definitely catty. But Lila wasn't really Lila here. She was Lila, Fake Fiancée. Almost like a superhero, playing a part.

"Absolutely. I'm thrilled to be here to be part of your wedding." A waiter set a glass of juice in front of her. "Actually, I'd love to hear details. It's so beautiful here. I can only imagine how wonderful your ceremony will be."

"The wedding's not here," Nanna said as she motioned for staff to serve breakfast. "It's at Julia's family's tiny vineyard."

She noted a little animosity there, but, again, none of her business. Particularly since Alonzo gazed at Julia with real love in his eyes. When he caught Julia's gaze, her lips rose in a smile filled with an equal amount of love. Julia might have dated Mitch, but she truly loved Alonzo.

Julia, Nanna and Mitch's mom, Marguerite, began to talk nonstop about the wedding. There was a gala tonight, hosted by the Ochoa family. Then on Friday night, Julia's parents would host an outdoor cocktail party. The Ochoas would host a second ball a few days before the wedding for out-of-town guests who hadn't been in Spain for the first ball. A few days later, the bride and fifty or so of her closest friends and relatives would have a luncheon as a bachelorette party. Alonzo and his groomsmen and fifty or so of his closest friends would have a bachelor party. And, of course, the Ochoas would host a rehearsal dinner the night before the actual wedding.

Lila's head spun. No wonder Mitch and Riccardo had advised her to get so many dresses and gowns. She'd thought they'd exaggerated. Now she wondered if she'd bought enough.

Mitch lost Lila for the entire day. Pacing the sitting room, waiting for her to dress for the welcome gala, he admitted to himself that he knew why. While his mom stayed behind to supervise preparations for tonight's ball, Julia, Lila and Nanna had taken one of the family limos into town to pick up her gown. Julia had kept them out all day. She also had been dropped at her family's small vineyard first. Then Nanna and

Lila had spent another thirty minutes returning to Ochoa Vineyards, and that left Lila only about an hour to dress.

Why?

Because Julia wanted to be the prettiest girl at the ball and she knew Lila could give her a real run for her money.

He shook his head in disbelief. Who'd have ever thought beautiful Julia would be jealous of Lila? His mousy assistant?

He was about to laugh when Lila's door finally opened and she walked out of her room in a red dress that almost made his eyes pop. Low cut and cruising her breasts to her waist like a second skin, the gown belled out into a skirt that wasn't full, but held yards and yards of material that swished when she walked.

She glanced down at herself. "Too risqué?"

"No!" Sweet mother of God. Who was this woman? How had he not noticed his assistant was so sexy?

He frowned. He hadn't noticed because he'd never seen her anywhere but work. She'd planned every one of his parties but she'd never attended any of them. For all he knew, the office might be the only place she dressed down. And why not? They were working.

She walked over to him, the satin of her ruby-red dress swishing, the pale skin of her shoulders shiny in the glow of the lamp by the sofa, her gray eyes sparkling.

She leaned in. Speaking in a conspiratorial tone, she said, "I have to admit I love this dress."

A floral scent hit him. Her shampoo. *His assistant's* shampoo. Something he'd smelled a million times. A wave of recognition looped through him, but as quickly as the connection came it floated away.

"You look wonderful in that dress."

She reached up and smoothed the collar of his tux jacket and straightened his bow tie. "*You* look wonderful." She gave him a quick, approving once-over, then glanced up at him again. "I like you in a tux."

His breath stuttered, confusing him. Lots of women told him that he looked good in a tux.

Yet for some reason hearing her say it stopped his heart and caused his nerve endings to crackle.

He stepped back, cleared his throat and shook his head slightly to force himself to return to the real world, where he had to fool his family and keep the focus on Julia and Alonzo.

Though he would have liked to ask her a million questions, this was one time they absolutely couldn't be late. He motioned to the door. "Ready?"

She smiled broadly. "Sure. I don't think I've ever been to a party looking this pretty. It's going to be fun."

What she said and her tone of voice caused the connection between the woman in front of him and his dowdy assistant to click again. If only for a few seconds, she stopped being two different people. She was his assistant in costume. Lila in a pretty dress. So, it baffled him that thinking of her chatting up a few of his friends or his dad's acquaintances squeezed his chest with jealousy.

"You're not there to have fun. You are there to pretend to be in love with me."

She said, "Uh-huh," as she headed for the door.

He reached it two seconds before she did and opened it for her. The urge to remind her that she couldn't flirt with other guests surged again but he stopped it. He wasn't the jealous type. She wasn't really his fiancée. And he could keep her at his side to make sure she didn't ruin the ruse.

He stopped just before pulling the door closed behind them, a little embarrassed by his need to be in control. This was Lila. When he gave her a job, she did it. He did not have to micromanage her. He had nothing to worry about.

Except that she had a secret that caused her to negotiate a new job as her payback for pretending to be his fiancée.

She worked for a winery, but didn't drink.

His grandmother thought she was pregnant, and would probably ask her a million questions—

Unless she'd already asked them while they were out with Julia that afternoon?

As they reached the sidewalk that led to the main house, he took her hand. Warm and smooth, it fit nicely in his palm. "So…did Nanna ask you anything that I should know about?"

"Julia kind of monopolized the conversations."

He sniffed a laugh. That he believed. "So, Nanna didn't say anything while you were waiting for Julia to try on dresses?"

She looked thoughtful for a second, then said, "No. Nothing significant that I can remember."

"Did she ask about your past?"

"Yes." She winced. "I decided it best not to lie and I told her the truth."

Two feet away from the side door he'd been guiding Lila to, he stopped. "You did?"

She nodded. "Yes."

"And that truth is…"

"Pretty boring. Just stuff about me being in foster care." She laughed. "Which is why she accepted it so easily."

She took a few steps toward the French doors and servants opened them for her. Music from a string quartet poured out as Lila smiled at the doormen and began walking inside the house.

Mitch scrambled after her. He stepped into the

private entry just in time to watch Riccardo take Lila's hands. "I see you put our money to good use."

Lila laughed and did a quick turn. "Isn't it gorgeous? Would you believe I got it on a clearance rack?"

Riccardo tapped her nose. "You're not just good-looking. You're smart. That's why we love you."

A surge of a different kind of jealousy rose up in Mitch. Lila had always been more comfortable with Riccardo. Right now the easy way she spoke with him made Mitch angry.

"Don't toss too much praise her way. Remember she's leaving us when we get home."

Riccardo's happy, flirty expression deflated. "I forgot."

Lila shrugged. "It's for the best." She faced Mitch. "Shall we go in?"

Mitch took the few steps that separated them, caught her elbow and led her into the ballroom. They weren't late, but early guests had already begun to arrive. Julia and Alonzo would make an entrance once everyone was seated. Mitch's parents stood at the entry to the ballroom with Nanna, greeting guests.

"Can I get you a drink?" He pulled in a breath. Realizing his mistake, he added, "Orange juice? Club soda?"

She shook her head. "No," she said, her gaze slowly circling the room. "I don't want to be distracted. I want to remember all of this. It's so gorgeous."

He shoved his hands in his trouser pockets. "It is pretty. My mom has wonderful taste."

"She does." She faced him with a smile. "And she seems like a lovely person."

"She is."

"I guess I sort of knew that from the fact that you and Riccardo are such good people. Good people come from good parents."

Now he was talking to real Lila. Not the woman who was a mix of his assistant and his fake fiancée. But just plain Lila. The woman who was as loyal as anyone could be. The hard worker. The woman who'd grown up in foster

care. He'd never thought much about her per-
sonally. But tonight, watching her reaction to
his luxurious home, disgrace at his bad behav-
ior with her enveloped him.

She got along so well with Riccardo. Why had
he and Lila never become friends?

He quietly said, "I do know that I was lucky."

"In spite of the fact that my life is dull, I was
pretty lucky too. Not every foster kid finds a way
to make it through university." Her smile grew.
"And after a day with your former girlfriend, I
also think you dodged a big bullet with Julia."
She leaned in close. "But if you tell anyone I said
that, I'll deny it."

A laugh burst from him. Up until this trip, he'd
never seen her sense of humor but clearly she had
a great one. So maybe the serious way he attacked
his work had kept her from getting comfortable
with him?

As more and more guests filed into the ballroom, Lila said, "Okay, here's the way I see this.
You are the best man, second son, who probably
has to make one or two obligatory comments or

maybe a toast or something, then for the rest of this event your job is basically to have a good time."

He hadn't thought of it like that, but the assistant in Lila had looked at the situation and summed it up perfectly.

"*Sí.*"

"Okay, so that means no more serious talk. If you want to drink, go ahead. I'll make sure you don't say anything too far out of line or put a lampshade on your head."

"A lampshade on my head?"

"It's an old American expression for when somebody drinks too much and has such a good time they do foolish things."

He nodded but all the good feelings that had been welling up in him disappeared in a puff of smoke, as the truth poked its way into their good time again. She was funny here but he'd never seen her sense of humor in the office. She didn't drink. She wanted another job. She was leaving him. How was he supposed to be happy around her when there were so many unanswered questions?

Nanna swished her way over. Wearing a pale blue gown and long diamond earrings, she looked like the wealthy matriarch that she was. She greeted Lila first. "Darling, you look fantastic."

Lila said, "Thanks. You look amazing."

Nanna bowed slightly. "Thank you." She peered around. "So? What do you think?"

Mitch said, "Everything's beautiful."

Nanna batted a hand. "You're a man. Of course you say that." She faced Lila again. "What do *you* think?"

"I'm bowled over."

Nanna frowned. "And that's good?"

Lila laughed. "Yes. Very good."

"Sweetheart," Nanna said, laying a hand on Lila's forearm, "I left my small beaded bag on the table behind the receiving line. Could you sneak over and get it? I'd ask Mitch but he'd get drawn into the conversations with arriving guests, and we wouldn't see him again until dinner."

Lila said, "I'll be glad to."

The second she was out of earshot, Nanna turned to Mitch. "So did you ask her?"

"Ask her?"

"If she's pregnant."

Mitch groaned. "I haven't really had two minutes alone with her. Besides, you're the one she talked to today."

Nanna batted a hand. "She told me about the foster child experience. Very sad. But it made her resilient. She's a wonderful girl, but if she's pregnant you need to know."

"Maybe she's waiting until after the wedding to tell me, so she doesn't steal any of Julia's limelight."

The lie rolled off his tongue easily. But inside Mitch felt odd again. What if Lila *was* pregnant? She wanted a new job. Because she thought he wouldn't support her through her pregnancy? Because he was a businessman who only thought of work? Because he hadn't even known that beneath those glasses and dowdy clothes was a really beautiful woman, who was also very nice?

She returned with Nanna's bag. Nanna took it, leaned in and kissed Lila's cheek. "Thank you."

Lila said, "You're welcome."

Nanna turned and began talking to another guest, beside them.

Mitch stole a peek at Lila's flat tummy. She couldn't be pregnant... Could she? And if she was, did she intend to raise a child alone? In New York City, where everything cost a fortune? Would not having a dad for her baby bring up bad memories of her own childhood?

Wait. There had to be a dad. That was just plain biology. And Mitch couldn't assume the guy didn't want to be in his baby's life. He could want to be in the baby's life but for some reason Lila didn't want him there. Maybe he was a loser? Maybe he was a thug—

Mitch groaned internally. Now he was making up stories about an imaginary father for an as yet undocumented baby.

He had to get some answers.

Nanna redirected the couple she was speaking with to Mitch and Lila, introducing Lila as his fiancée. She played her role, leaning toward him so he could put his arm around her waist.

They spent the next twenty minutes talking

to guests that Nanna directed to them. Julia and Alonzo arrived to a blare of trumpets—undoubtedly Julia's idea—then dinner was served. He and Lila sat at a long table with Alonzo and Julia, his parents, her parents and the entire wedding party. There wasn't a second of privacy to ask the questions nagging at him, but even if there had been, Mitch had the sudden, uncomfortable feeling that he couldn't ask for such personal information from somebody he barely knew.

He wasn't bold to the point of almost being illmannered like Nanna.

He wasn't friendly with Lila the way Riccardo was.

He wasn't anything.

She might be in trouble, real trouble, and though Mitch had worked with her for a year, he didn't know her well enough to help her.

He wasn't sure if he should be ashamed of himself or mad at himself.

His father made the first toast. Julia's father made the second. Then Julia's mother declined a toast, dabbing tears from her eyes and saying Julia's dad had said it all. Mitch's mom was ready with a fabulous salute to her older son, then everybody looked at Mitch.

He rose. He'd been thinking about this for weeks before this trip, so he very casually picked up his champagne glass and said, "To Alonzo and Julia, the perfect couple. May they have a long, happy marriage. *Salud.*"

Everyone said, *"Salud!"* and took a drink of champagne.

When he was seated again, Lila touched his arm. "That was perfect."

"I decided to think of myself as just an ordinary best man for my brother and gave the toast that way."

"Well, you were brilliant."

His father announced dancing, and Alonzo and Julia immediately took to the floor. After a first dance for the about-to-be-weds, Mitch rose. "Our family goes out onto the dance floor immediately to signal to the other guests that they can dance."

As he helped Lila stand, she said, "Sounds great."

They danced the first dance a little stiff and awkward but by the second, they were much more attuned to each other. His hand on the small of her back relaxed. The hand she had on his shoulder shifted to be more comfortable.

His nervousness settled. Lila was a great dancer. Very light on her feet. Very easy to guide around the dance floor.

When the second song started, Riccardo cut in. Polite, Mitch smiled and excused himself, but he stood on the sidelines watching her as Riccardo whirled her around in a huge, looping circle to the music of the waltz that floated around them. She tossed her head back and laughed, and the weird jealousy rolled through him again.

As soon as the song ended, he was at her side. "Thanks, cuz. We'll see you later."

Riccardo excused himself and walked away, but the second the music started Lila was in Mitch's arms again.

"So what were you laughing about with Riccardo?"

"He offered to give me his condo if I'd stay with Ochoa Online."

The possibility that she wouldn't leave filled him with bubbly joy. "And you said?"

"No!" She laughed and he whirled her around again.

"Why don't you want to work for us anymore?"

"Maybe the better question to be asking yourself is where am I getting Lila a job?"

"But Riccardo and I want you to stay."

"Really? Because if I stay then all bets are off and I'm not your fiancée anymore and you've got some explaining to do to your nanna."

"I know you think you're very clever at confusing me. But I've caught you every time, and you've just been lucky with the plane landing, or Nanna insisting I chat with her or being late for breakfast."

He yanked her close, tight up against his body to show her that he was in control, and instantly regretted it. She felt wonderful. How could he make a point when he was tongue-tied?

"Don't forget Julia keeping us out all day."

Her soft, breathless voice did something to his soul. She was as turned on as he was. Though she used her wit to try to divert his attention, he could feel the quiver that ran through her small frame.

He smiled. This was a game he could play. "Julia thinks you're beautiful."

She caught his gaze. "No, she doesn't."

"Why else did she keep you out all day except to limit the time you had to prepare for the gala?" He whirled them around again. "But you fooled her. You didn't need three hours of prep work to be beautiful."

The song ended. He kept her pressed against him, staring into her eyes. "You are beautiful tonight. More beautiful than she is."

Her eyes shifted, softened. But she said, "Music has stopped."

"So? We're in love, remember?" He dipped his head slowly, desperately wanting a kiss, desperately curious about what she'd do if he kissed her for real, not a quick brush of a goodbye kiss.

Everything around them melted away. She studied his eyes, her own pale gray orbs curious, but wary. She wanted the kiss as much as he did, but something held her back.

She pulled away. "I think I need a club soda."

He released her, but took her hand and headed for the bar. As much as he wanted to kiss her—really kiss her—the fact that she'd stepped away told him that he couldn't until he knew what was going on with her. Was she pregnant? Was that why she wanted another job?

He already knew he couldn't ask her something so personal, so private until he really got to know her. She'd slid out of every chance to have a conversation, but she wasn't wiggling out this time. There were no parties, no galas scheduled for Thursday night. Tomorrow, there'd be no one to save her.

# CHAPTER FIVE

LILA WOKE THE next morning with plenty of time to spare before the family breakfast. She showered, fixed her hair, put on makeup and slid into a comfortable skirt and silky top. When she stepped out into the sitting room, Mitch was at the table in the small kitchenette, his tablet in front of him. He was probably online, reading the morning news. The delicious aroma of fresh coffee permeated the small space. So did the scent of toast.

"Good morning." She carefully walked through the seating area to the little round table with four chairs. She wasn't exactly sure what had happened the night before, but her heart tripped over itself when she remembered that minute on the dance floor when she was absolutely positive he was going to kiss her. She'd called herself all kinds of crazy for even thinking he'd wanted to kiss her. But she couldn't discount the fact that something had sizzled between them, and now the mood in their apartment felt different.

He smiled at her. "Good morning."

He wasn't just smiling. There was a weird gleam in his eyes.

Her heart bumped against her ribs. Something absolutely, positively had changed.

"Nanna called. No family breakfast this morning." He pointed to a silver coffeepot. "The cook sent up coffee and a tray of cheeses and breads for toast."

"Oh."

"Nanna has an appointment with her stylist today to figure out her hairdo for the wedding."

Lila couldn't help it; she laughed.

"What?"

"It's funny to hear you talk about girl things."

"I know about girl things."

Oh, she would bet he did. But she wasn't opening that door. Instead, she picked up a coffee cup and poured herself a mug of the hot, dark liquid from the silver carafe. She set the cup on the table and was about to pull out a chair, but hesitated when she saw the wicked gleam in his eyes again. That's when she put two and two together and realized that no family breakfast and Nanna leaving for hours on an errand meant she would be alone with Mitch. Maybe all morning.

"So what's your mom doing?"

The light in his eyes intensified. "Worried you'll have to spend time with me?"

Heat rose to her cheeks.

"Well, don't. We have a board meeting at eight. My mom has to attend, so Nanna invited you to go with her and help her decide on a hairdo."

The breath returned to her lungs. "I can do that."

His head tilted as he looked at her, studying her hair. "Last week, I might have wondered if you could." He smiled again. "Today, I know you can."

The way he kept looking at her, smiling at her, sent a ripple of unease through her.

He rose from the table. "These meetings fre-

quently last all day." He headed for the door. "I'm
assuming you and Nanna will have lunch in town
and probably shop. Riccardo said you still have
the credit cards." He glanced over at her. "Use
them. And don't bargain hunt. I want Nanna to
see you spending my money as if you're accustomed to it."

"Okay."

"Okay." He turned to the door, then faced her
again. "And don't worry about missing me while
I'm busy. I've arranged for us to have a private
dinner, here, in the apartment tonight."

Lila's breath froze. Private dinner? She remembered those thirty seconds when he'd yanked her
against him on the dance floor. The sizzle. The
confusion.

And the longing.

She fought the urge to squeeze her eyes shut.
She'd had a crush on this man forever. When he'd
pulled her so close—well, her thoughts had spun
out of control and she'd felt so many wonderful
things.

What if he'd felt them too?

Oh, boy.

The words *private dinner* took on a whole new meaning.

But he opened the door and was gone before Lila could blink let alone argue. She straightened her shoulders. She wasn't going to fall into the trap of thinking he intended to seduce her. They'd shared one "crackly" moment the night before. He hadn't instantly fallen in love with her. He probably wanted to have dinner alone so he could catch her up on whatever happened at their family business meeting that day.

She was, after all, his assistant—

No, she wasn't. She'd quit his employ. Anything his family decided for the company today made no difference to her.

There was only one reason left for his wanting private time with her. One logical, part of the charade reason: he wanted her to tell him things about her past.

After the way he'd looked at her the night before—

The way he'd smiled at her all morning—

There was something going on in that Ochoa brain of his. He definitely had a plan for getting her to spill the beans she'd kept to herself for an entire year in his employ. And he seemed pretty cocky about it. Which meant he had an idea that he genuinely believed would work to get her to talk.

The phone in the sitting area rang. She set her coffee on the table and raced to get it, hoping it was Mitch telling her he'd only been teasing about the private dinner, or he'd changed his mind, or something had come up that meant they wouldn't be alone.

Because the one thing she hadn't factored into this charade was that they'd be alone. Somehow she'd always pictured them at parties and family dinners, or dressing for parties and family dinners.

The phone rang again and she picked up the receiver and cautiously said, "Hello?"

"It's me. Nanna. I'm just calling to let you know I'm already in the limo. Breakfast by myself takes a lot less time than with family."

Lila squeezed her eyes shut. She was not getting out of a private dinner with Mitch. "I'll be right there."

After grabbing her purse from her bedroom, Lila raced down the stairs and outside where she found the family limo sitting in front of the duplex. A driver opened the door for her and she slid inside.

Smiling at Nanna, she said, "Good morning."

"Good morning." Nanna squeezed her hand. "We're going to have such fun." She leaned in and whispered, "You got a credit card from Mitch, right?"

She laughed. Two minutes in Nanna's company and she already felt better. "Yes. And he said to use it."

"That's my boy."

The driver started the limo and pulled out.

"Once we get this hair nonsense out of the way, we'll have lunch—then we can shop."

Lila laughed again. She should have felt guilty about using Mitch's money or maybe her pride should have stopped her from buying a skirt, two blouses and a new pair of shoes, but Nanna made it very easy to get into the role of playing fiancée to her grandson. Nanna was inordinately happy that Mitch was happy. All in all, they had a great day.

But ten minutes into the drive back to the vineyard, Nanna said, "So, aside from what you told me yesterday about your childhood, what else do I need to know about you?"

"Actually, I pretty much told you everything." Lila shrugged. "There's not much to know about me."

Nanna turned her rich, dark eyes on Lila. "Really?"

"I have an uncomplicated past. I grew up, went to university, got a job." She smiled at Nanna, but Nanna didn't smile back. "Honestly. There's not much to tell."

"I believe there is much to tell," Nanna contradicted. "But I think you look around and see a world beyond yours and assume we wouldn't be interested."

Now *that* was perceptive. No wonder Mitch

worried about her figuring out the ruse. "That's part of it."

"And maybe you compare yourself to Julia?"

Lila winced. For as much as she knew Nanna was digging for something, she also couldn't lie to her. She doubted anyone could lie to her. The woman should work for the CIA. "I try not to compare myself to Julia. We're clearly two different people. I think comparing us would be a big mistake."

"Yes. Mostly because New York changed Mitch. For the better. His taste in women certainly improved."

"That's not really fair to Julia."

"Julia is a lovely woman." Nanna straightened the pleats in her skirt. "But she is also complicated." She met Lila's gaze. "I'm sure you can figure that out from the switch in choice of brothers. She loved Mitch, but she also loved the fact that his older brother would someday run the family business."

"Ah."

"Ah, indeed." Nanna took a quick breath. "But

I have no doubt now that she loves Alonzo." She shook her head. "Complicated."

"Love usually is."

"And you believe Mitcham is over her?"

Lila laughed slightly. "Absolutely. In fact, he's happy for Julia and Alonzo. You should see the lengths he was willing to go to to make sure the focus of these two weeks was on his brother and future bride. This is their time. He wants them to enjoy the celebrations."

"He told you that?"

"Yes, he did."

Nanna studied Lila's eyes for a few seconds. "He trusts you."

Those terrible feelings about deceiving Nanna rose in Lila again, but she wasn't really deceiving her. Mitch really did trust her. That's why they were in this charade. Talking about trust wasn't lying.

"Yes. He trusts me with a lot more than you'd ever believe."

Nanna squeezed her hand. "That's good. After the mess with him finding Alonzo and Julia, he needs to be with someone he trusts."

That nudged a little bit of guilt into her thoughts. But when Lila weighed the pros and cons, and considered how this one little charade really had assured this celebration would be about Julia and Alonzo, she couldn't feel too guilty.

The limo pulled up to the apartment building first. Nanna kissed Lila's cheek before Lila slid out of the car. The driver handed her purchases to her, and happy after the fun day with Nanna, she all but skipped up the stairs. Until she remembered she was having a private dinner with Mitch.

Damn it.

She walked up the rest of the steps slowly. They were a good hour away from dinner. Mitch could still be at his family's meeting. She could use the time for a bubble bath and to dress.

And then—

Then she would do what needed to be done. It wasn't like they would be out in public where she had to play a role. Actually, that was the first sane thought she'd had about this time alone. Technically, she was working out a two-week notice. In fact, with this dinner being private, she shouldn't be Lila, Fake Fiancée. She should be Lila, Mitch's assistant.

The very thought that she should be herself put a spring back in her step. Mitch wasn't curious about that woman—his assistant—or attracted to her. She'd spent tons of time alone with him as his assistant and he'd barely looked at her.

She raced into the apartment, tossed her new things on her bed and got into the shower instead of a bubble bath. She washed her hair, intending to let it frizz out again, but the straightener the beautician had used was doing the job it promised to do for the next sixty days. Her hair, even after using a blow-dryer, was sleek and shiny.

She really shouldn't have put on makeup, but she liked the way she looked with a little mascara and eyeliner. And a dab of lip gloss wasn't a sin.

Luckily, she did have a pair of her old jeans— but, darn it, she really wanted to wear one of her new blouses.

But she wasn't putting on shoes.

And she wasn't wearing her contacts.

A few minutes after she entered the sitting

room, a member of the kitchen staff arrived with dinner. She was about to tell him Mitch hadn't come back from his meeting when he stepped out of his bedroom, pulling a polo shirt over his head, looking freshly showered. He also wore jeans. His feet were bare. He intended to be as comfortable as she was.

"Thank you, Tomas," he said, indicating that Tomas could roll the cart containing dinner and wine into the kitchenette area, near the table.

Tomas did as he was told and exited with a smile and a quick nod.

Amazed, Lila watched him go, then faced Mitch again. "You have some wicked good staff."

"We pride ourselves on knowing how to pick excellent employees. It's why we don't usually expect them to ask us to find them a new job."

Wow. Direct hit. Right for the jugular.

She sucked in a breath. "These are special circumstances."

"I gathered that."

He motioned for her to join him at the table, then he took the two covered dishes off the cart and set them at the two place settings. He removed the lids, revealing steak and potatoes.

"Smells good."

"It should be. Our chef trained all over Europe before he finally settled in to work for our restaurant."

"Nice."

She took her seat and he sat across from her. "I expected to see more surprise from you at how we live."

She shrugged. "You forget that I see how you and Riccardo live in New York. Plus, I'm playing your fiancée. I'm supposed to know you enough that how you live doesn't surprise me." She paused for a second, then said, "Nanna and I had another bit of a conversation today. She appreciates that you trust me."

"I do trust you." He plunged his fork into his steak. "Did you tell her anything I need to know?"

"No. I've pretty much been able to keep the conversations neutral and simple, focused on a few main facts."

* * *

Frustration rolled through Mitch. If direct and outspoken Nanna couldn't get Lila to talk, he wondered if he'd be able to. Still, the purpose of this dinner was to get to know her so that eventually she'd tell him why she wanted to leave his employ, why she didn't drink and if she was pregnant.

The best way to get her to open up would be to talk to her, to let a personal conversation evolve naturally. Let it ebb. Let it flow. Let a little trust in him build for her—the way he trusted her.

"So in spite of the fact that you were able to keep your secrets from Nanna, I take it you had fun with her."

"The woman's a shopping machine."

He laughed. "And you spent money?"

She pointed at her blouse. "This shirt's new. And it set you back more than my part of the month's rent."

"That's right. You share an apartment. With your friend Sally?"

She glanced up, surprised.

"I heard you telling Riccardo you would be taking a friend shopping with you the day before we left."

The way she could talk to Riccardo rankled, but he smiled. After all, he was trying to get this woman to trust him the way he trusted her. He couldn't get mad that she was closer to his cousin. That's what he was trying to fix.

"You mentioned her name was Sally."

"Actually, Sally got a promotion about a year ago and can now afford her own apartment."

"Oh." And maybe that was the reason for her sudden interest in a new job?

Before he could ask, she said, "My roommates are Joselyn and Jennie." She laughed. "I call them the two jays. Like blue jays only two jays." She shook her head. "I have a weird sense of humor."

He cut into his steak. "No. I just think your mind is always working."

"That's one way to put it."

The conversation died as they began to eat. She took a bite of her steak and groaned. "Holy cow."

He leaned in. "The chef's secret ingredient is butter."

Her eyes rose to meet his. That's when he noticed she was wearing her glasses. He was making the connection between her as his assistant and her as his fake fiancée so completely that he hadn't even noticed her glasses. Right now, she was just Lila. Something of a cross between the two.

"Your chef adds butter to meat that's already loaded with fat?"

"I know. Decadent, isn't it?"

"Yeah. But it's also probably ten million calories."

He cleared his throat. Knowing what he was about to ask her was personal, and she'd probably shut him down, he nonetheless said, "You don't look like the kind of woman who has to watch her weight."

She laughed. "All women watch their weight."

Her laughter thrilled him. She'd laughed with him before. Especially when she was dressed up and pretending to be somebody else. But this woman was the real Lila and she was laughing with him.

"Hell of a cross to bear," he said, teasing her, hoping she wouldn't disappear back into the protective shell of the character she was supposed to be playing.

"Yeah, especially when your fiancé serves you steak slathered in butter."

He liked the way she very casually called him her fiancé. Maybe he was getting accustomed to that too?

"Tell me a bit about growing up in foster care."

"I already told you I don't care to revisit all that. Why don't you tell me more about growing up here? Now that I've seen your home and met your family, I'll have a better perspective."

He set his fork down. This dinner was supposed to be about getting to know her and she'd already turned the tables. But what if part of getting her to trust him was respecting her wishes? She didn't want to talk about her years in foster care. Who could blame her? And she did want to hear about his childhood.

"All right. When my dad and his brother inherited the vineyard, they also bought the adjoining vineyard, not just to increase the business enough to support two families, but also to have a second residence."

She put her elbow on the table and her chin on her fist, watching him as he spoke. "That's how you and Riccardo became so close? You grew up next door to each other."

"We grew up together. My mom and my aunt basically ran the business office, and the stories go that Riccardo and I were in the same play yard between their two desks."

She smiled. "Your moms didn't want to be away from you or have you raised by a babysitter. That's kinda nice."

"I never thought of it that way before, but, *sí*. It probably was nice."

He could see a shadow of sadness in her eyes and ached to ask her about her own childhood, but knew it was nowhere near as pleasant as his, and suddenly he understood her hesitancy to talk about it. Who would want to relive loneliness? Pain?

"So," he said, picking up his fork again, deciding to continue talking about himself, about good times, so that maybe she could live them through him. "By the time we were six or eight, we behaved more like twins than cousins. We worked alongside each other in the vineyards when we were teens, and had desks in the same room when we began our internships in the office."

As he took a bite of steak, she said, "That makes sense. And also explains how well you click for Ochoa Online."

"Technically, we've been working together for decades."

Her smile warmed. "That's wonderful."

"Or you could say our dads took advantage of slave labor."

That made her laugh. "It was good to be together so much. It bonded you. Made you the great team you are today."

"Yes." And he could see that she envied that. Or maybe longed for it. He felt the empty hole in her life as surely as if it were a living, breathing thing.

"What about Christmas?"

He glanced over at her. "What about Christmas?"

"With all this togetherness, your family Christmas must be happy." Her smile grew. "Wonderful."

He pulled in a breath. He'd never really thought about it. But he supposed that to an outsider, someone who was totally alone, being surrounded by so much family must be wonderful. "Riccardo's family and our family have separate celebrations for some things. But everybody likes to be with Nanna, so Christmas Eve is in her quarters. Christmas dinner is in my parents'."

She nodded. "Nice."

"Really. It is." And he now regretted whining about having to fly to Spain for the holidays last year when she might not have had anywhere at all to go.

Knowing he had to get them out of this weird mood, he said, "Okay, so you don't want to discuss your childhood...and I respect that. But surely you've got a good story or two from university."

She thought about that. "The whole reason I made it through was that the coffee shop I worked for paid well and had great benefits. They also paid a big portion of my tuition."

His heart lifted a bit for her. "That was a lucky break."

"Yes. That was when I began to see that in some respects I was lucky."

Being a foster child did not make her lucky. Having one good life break also did not make her lucky. Yet her tone of voice said she believed she was.

His curiosity rose and he peeked at her. "How so?"

"No matter where I worked or who I roomed with, I was able to make friends. I was always able to find friends."

He leaned forward, across the table, putting his elbow close to hers and his chin on his fist, mimicking her. "Why am I not surprised?"

"You should be surprised. In an entire year this

is our first real conversation. You obviously think I'm a real dolt."

"Maybe I'm the dolt who never thought to ask you anything personal?"

"Personal things don't belong in the workplace."

"Yes, but you went out of your way for me. A lot." He leaned a little closer; the desire to kiss her once again swam through his veins. This time it was stronger, more powerful. She wasn't just Lila, his confusing assistant. She wasn't Lila, his fake fiancée being sexy. She was both of those wrapped up in one cute little package with sleek hair and big glasses. And he liked her. He really liked her.

He leaned in a little closer. "I did notice what a good worker you were."

"But you never noticed me otherwise."

He leaned in a little more. "I'm noticing now."

Her tongue darted out and slid along her lips, but she didn't move. Maybe being together in a different situation than boss and assistant had changed her opinion of him too? Maybe it made her notice him as more than a boss?

He erased the final inches between them and pressed his lips to hers. Soft and warm, they melted under his touch. Desire slammed through him, but so did an aching frustration. How could he kiss her properly sitting down, with a table between them? Without breaking the contact of their mouths, he slid his hands behind her upper arms and pulled her up with him as he rose, taking the step that put them as close as they had been when they were dancing.

Then he deepened the kiss and unexpected awareness spiraled through him. This wasn't a woman he'd met in Central Park, at the theater or in a coffee shop.

This was Lila.

A woman he genuinely liked.

And he was kissing her.

It was the most different, most wonderful thing.

# CHAPTER SIX

LILA'S HEART HAMMERED in her chest. She had been Real Lila all through dinner, hoping to deter him. Instead, the opposite had happened. He seemed interested in her, bare feet, glasses and all. She had absolutely no idea what had happened, what *was* happening between them, but she'd had enough boyfriends, flirtations and relationships to know the man was interested in her.

The man she'd had a crush on for the past year wasn't just noticing her. He was interested.

Kissing her.

The warmth that filled her was part joy, part need. Then he deepened the kiss a second time, opening her mouth and sliding his tongue along the rough texture of hers, and her knees about buckled.

He was definitely interested in her.

The oddest thought drifted into her brain, wound around her nerve endings and whispered through her consciousness.

*What if this was her chance?*

What if fate had set her up as his fake fiancée not to get her a new job but to have a real chance with him? Yes, she wanted to find her mom, but she could do it as easily as his girlfriend as she could some nameless assistant working for another company. Maybe more easily. If she could get up her courage and tell him the truth about her past, maybe he could use his connections to help her?

Her breath stalled. But he pulled back slightly.

Raising his hands to the stems of her glasses, he said, "Let's get rid of these."

"Okay." Her voice came out a mere whisper, as horrible pain tumbled through her.

He'd asked her to take off her glasses. He didn't like *her*. He liked Fake Lila. He'd taken off the glasses to bring her back. If he wanted Fake Lila, she couldn't tell him the truth. She couldn't tell him anything.

Unless...

She looked down at the tortoiseshell frames on the table. Unless he was about to take them into no-glasses territory? The big romantic place. The place for which she wasn't prepared...

His bedroom.

All the wonderful warmth floating through her turned to the ice of fear. If he was only toying with her, or having some fun with Fake Lila, it would kill her to make love with him, and then be nothing to him when they got home. But even if he was getting feelings for her, this was too soon. She wasn't ready. But he wasn't either. He didn't know her. Not all of her. And unless she could say with absolute certainty that he was interested in Real Lila, not Fake Lila, she couldn't tell him. She most certainly couldn't go to his bedroom with him.

She took a step back, cleared her throat and looked him in the eye, as much as she could without her thick glasses.

"We have a big day tomorrow with Julia's parents' garden party." She took another step back.

"So I'm going to go." She picked up her glasses and motioned to her bedroom. "I want to make sure I get enough sleep."

His head tilted as if she'd confused him.

Okay. They were even then because he'd sure as hell confused her.

She turned and walked back to her bedroom with as much grace and dignity as she could muster. Behind the safety of her closed door, she slipped out of her skirt and blouse and into her Giants T-shirt and pajama pants.

But sleep didn't come.

She tried for an hour, wishing she had someone to talk to, then realized that she did. She might not have a close friend in Spain, but she had plenty of friends in New York. And it was still daytime there.

Grabbing her cell phone, she hit contacts and dialed Sally's number. Though she was probably at work, she answered in three rings.

"So how's life in the fast lane?"

"A lot faster than I thought it was going to be."

Sally sighed greedily. "Tell me everything."

Lila sat up in bed, plumped her pillows and plunged into a discussion of Nanna and Julia, balls and shopping.

"Oh, my gosh!" Sally's voice dripped with incredulity. "That's unbelievable."

"Okay, then. If you think that's unbelievable, you're gonna faint at this."

"I am on the edge of my chair."

"He kissed me."

"He? Mitch? Isn't he supposed to kiss you to make the ruse work?"

"Yes. But that's only in public. He kissed me in private tonight."

"What in the heck is happening between you two?"

"That's the big question." She paused, bit her lower lip. "I kinda dressed like Real Lila for dinner tonight, except that I like the way mascara looks and a little lip gloss never killed anyone. So I was a cross between Real Lila and Fake Lila."

"You're enjoying this! You don't want to be a mouse anymore."

"I just… I don't know. I guess I never realized

mascara and pretty blouses could make such a big difference. Especially with my hair all sleek."

"And you like new Lila."

"I'm not really new. It's still me, except pretty."

"You were always pretty. You just hid it."

She sighed. "I suppose."

"So if you're enjoying this and the guy you swoon over kissed you, what's the problem?"

"He took off my glasses when we were kissing."

"And?"

"And it makes me feel that either he doesn't like to be reminded of the real me or he was going to take us a little further than I was ready to go."

Sally's "Oh…" came out slow and strangled. "You're in the big leagues."

"I guess."

"And it happened too fast?"

"We've only been here a few days."

"I get that. But technically you've known him for a year."

"I know him, but he doesn't know me."

They were silent for a few seconds, then Sally said, "You can't tell him about your mom?"

"I could… I *would* if I knew he was interested in me. For real. But I won't humiliate myself by telling the story to someone when it doesn't really matter."

"So what are you going to do?"

Lila laughed. "Call you?"

"For advice. Hmmm." Sally paused, obviously considering how to answer. "I think that if he only likes Fake Lila you're right to back off."

"That's my thought too."

"Now, don't be ready to jump ship yet. There's another side to this. If you really are sliding into a combination of Fake Lila and Real Lila, then you just have to make sure he slides with you. Then you can tell him. Then he'll know you, and everything else is going to depend on whether or not he's genuinely interested or just being a player."

"I forgot what a serial dater he is."

"Yeah," Sally said, obviously still thinking. "But all men date around until the right girl catches their attention."

"You think I'm the right girl for him?"

"You don't?"

She had. From the first moment she laid eyes on him, she had. She sighed heavily, almost afraid to admit it, afraid to jinx what was happening between them. "I do."

"Then keep wearing your glasses. Not all the time, but in your downtime. If it's you he likes, he'll adjust to Real Lila, and you'll know it. Then you can tell him about your mom. And if he doesn't adjust? Then maybe *you* don't want *him*."

The following evening, Mitch sat in the sitting area of his small apartment, waiting for Lila. He knew she'd talked to his grandmother about what to wear to this outdoor cocktail party, but he didn't think she had to worry. She seemed to have impeccable taste. Or at least the knowledge of what looked good on her because she'd been stunning him since the day she got out of the limo at the airport.

And that kiss? It had been amazing.

But he had no idea what he was doing with her. First, she didn't really talk to him. She very well could be pregnant, yet she hadn't felt the need to tell him and he still didn't feel comfortable asking. Then there was the matter of her wanting another job. All along, he'd had a ping that something was terribly wrong with that. If she was pregnant, maybe a new job had something to do with affording a baby. But he and Riccardo could provide both money and moral support. So why was she leaving them?

Still, the biggest reason of all to be careful was that he didn't want to hurt her. He'd been horribly surprised by Julia falling in love with Alonzo. True, it all sorted out for him very quickly, but there was no place in a Spaniard's life for weakness. And with the abundance of potential dates in New York City, he'd happily realized he never had to get serious about a woman again.

Which meant, if he got involved with Lila, their relationship wouldn't last. It would end. And he would hurt her.

He shouldn't have kissed her.

She had been right to step away and go to her room.

So how did he get this charade back on track

and still nose into her personal life—on the chance that he could help her if she was pregnant?

He wasn't sure he could.

Her bedroom door opened. She stepped out wearing a yellow dress and light-colored sandals, not quite white but not quite yellow either. Her hair had been pinned up on one side.

She pointed at it. "This is my nod toward the fact that the party is outside."

"You look—" Perfect. Fantastic. Unreal. So wonderful he wanted to bite her neck, and make her laugh and moan at the same time.

He sucked in a breath, reminding himself that if she was pregnant, he wanted to help her, and he couldn't help her if he romanced her then dumped her. But pregnancy aside, they were here to ensure his brother and future sister-in-law were the stars of this wedding celebration.

They had a charade to pull off. And he had to make sure she would do her part.

"You look very nice."

She peered at him. "That's it? Very nice?"

He laughed. "All right. You look spectacular.

You've been surprising me every day of this trip."
He suddenly realized the one thing that would get
her totally on board again. Her reward. The reason she'd agreed to do this. "In fact, you're helping me so much that I can't even tell you how
grateful I am. So I think it might be time you and
I talk about the new job you want."

"Now?"

He pointed to the door. "I'll need details on
things like the kind of work you want to do, how
much salary you want, benefits—" He said that,
then paused, giving her the chance to say, "Yeah,
I'm going to need good benefits with a baby on
the way." But she didn't take the bait. "So that I
can take a look at my friend list and call their HR
departments to see who needs someone."

"Okay."

He caught her gaze. "You know. This is the kind
of task I'd normally give to you."

She looked down. "I'm kind of busy right now."

The urge to put his finger under her chin and
lift her face was nearly irresistible, and he was
glad he'd started this conversation. Leaving him

made her as unhappy as the thought of her leaving made him. There was hope that he could persuade her to stay in his employ—with a raise—and then he could help her. He just had to tread lightly.

They had the limo to themselves because his parents and Nanna had gone to the vineyard an hour earlier to spend time with Julia's parents to discuss last-minute details of the wedding.

He said very little on the drive, satisfied that he had her thinking about how she would miss working with him and Riccardo. If he gave her some space to really ponder that, she might recognize keeping her current job was the right thing to do.

They arrived at Julia's parents' vineyard, and as she stepped out she gasped. "Oh, my goodness. It's so homey."

He laughed. "Is that another way of saying small?"

"You may not notice this, mister," she said, following his lead when he gestured with his hand that she should walk around the side of the stately stone house to the back patio. "But your family's estate is a little commercial."

"We do sell wine there."

"And I think that's all you ever think about."

"Sometimes I think about selling golf balls."

She laughed and shook her head. "You're incorrigible."

"But you like me."

She stopped. Her gaze crawled up to his. "Yes. And I'm not sure what that says about me."

He started to laugh, but he remembered he wasn't supposed to flirt with her when they were alone. It was so easy to romance her that he had to remind himself to fight the impulse.

Then her words soaked in and his mouth turned down. *She didn't want to like him?* That was more than a little insulting. Especially since he wasn't sure if she was talking about liking him romantically or liking him as a boss.

She walked away and he scrambled to catch up with her.

"Why did you say that?"

"What?"

"That you didn't know what it said about you that you liked me."

"You're a very demanding man. Yet that doesn't seem to bother me."

Good. Sort of. He didn't want them to be flirting, but how insulting was it that she didn't want to like him as a boss? Especially when he was trying to keep her as an employee.

"You're my assistant. You're supposed to do what I ask." They walked into the crowd of about a hundred well-dressed people, milling around a beautiful blue pool. Waiters served appetizers and drinks. He hailed one who brought a tray of champagne.

He took a flute and said, "A glass of club soda for my fiancée, please."

Lila turned to him with a smile. "Let's not fight about how bossy you are. Let's enjoy the evening."

She was back to being logical Lila, ace assistant, who didn't like him.

He studied his champagne, brooding because he'd never guessed she didn't like his bossiness— because he was her employer. He was supposed to be bossy.

Apparently, none of this bothered her because she studied the crowd like Cinderella at her first ball.

"So is that why you want to leave Ochoa On-line?"

She faced him. "No. Not really. There was never a time when I didn't think I could handle you."

The waiter came with her club soda. Mitch took it from the tray, handing it to her just as Julia's parents spotted them and raced over.

Rosa kissed his cheek first, then homed in on Lila. Taking her hands, she said, "I am happy to see Mitch has finally met his match."

Lila smiled gracefully, then glanced up at him lovingly. "I am too."

The joke wasn't lost on Julia's dad, David. He laughed and hugged Lila. "I've heard you're a firecracker."

From Julia, no doubt, who'd already criticized Lila's choice of clothes for breakfast and kept her away from home so long she barely had time to dress for the first gala.

"Where *are* the bride and groom?" Mitch said,

not caring if either of her parents caught that he knew it had been Julia who'd been talking about Lila.

"Milling about," Rosa said. A flood of people had accumulated behind them, so she added, "Go. Have fun. We'll work our way back to you once all the guests have been greeted."

He smiled and nodded, but as he directed Lila away, he said, "You know what? I should be thanking my lucky stars Julia picked Alonzo. I never had the warm fuzzies for her family."

Lila laughed. "Warm fuzzies?"

He waved his hand. "Or whatever it is you Americans say."

"We say *warm fuzzies*. I've just never heard it coming from *you*."

"Maybe I'm changing." Or maybe he needed to. She'd said her reason for wanting to leave his employ wasn't his bossiness, but it certainly couldn't hurt to be a more diplomatic boss.

She shook her head. "You don't want to change."

He looked into her eyes. Soft, gray orbs that were always filled with emotion. Right now, they oozed warmth. Why had he never noticed that? "Really?"

"No. You're good just the way you are."

*Then why do you want to work for someone else?*

He wanted to ask her. He really did. He wasn't afraid of the answer until he realized that he would fix whatever she said. He'd totally change the way his office ran—

To keep an assistant?

Or to keep Lila?

Because he was beginning to like her?

*Really like her?*

They finally reached the table where his mom sat with Nanna while his dad stood beside them, talking to another vintner.

Lila immediately walked to Nanna and leaned down to hug her. "You look stunning." Nanna's pale blue dress enhanced the gray in her salt-and-pepper hair but somehow made her look years younger.

"Doesn't she?" Mitch's mom said.

Nanna batted a hand. "With money, even an

old coot can look good." She motioned for Lila
to take the seat beside her, and she did.

Then Nanna glanced up at him. "Oh, Mitcham.
I'm sorry. I didn't see you."

He would have teased her, except he sort of
understood. This new version of Lila seemed to
always steal the show. Not because she was ex-
ceptional, but because she was kind and warm.
She didn't overdress, wanting people to notice
her. She didn't laugh too loud, edge her way into
conversations.

She was just easy to be with.

He suddenly realized why the charade was
working so well. She fit. She fit into his family.
She fit with him.

He took a step back. The collar of his white
shirt got unbearably tight.

Oh, dear God.

Had he actually met his match?

He didn't want a match! He liked being single.
Being free.

Julia and Alonzo strolled over. Wearing a pale
pink cocktail dress, with her black hair piled on

top of her head in an array of curls, Julia was stunning. When she reached Mitch, he hugged her, but the familiarity of the hug drove a tsunami of memories through his brain. The strangest truth rumbled through him, surprising him. Julia had been his girlfriend forever, but Alonzo had been able to swoop in and steal her because he'd been the crappiest boyfriend under the sun. He'd gone on business trips, leaving her behind. He'd constantly canceled dates because of work. Eventually, she'd had it with him and had taken up with his brother. A man who treated her very, very well. Who didn't put the business before her. Who wasn't trying to conquer the world. A man who wasn't selfish.

A man who only had to run one vineyard—he didn't have to assure the financial security of his entire family.

The thought brought him up short. He wasn't a bad boyfriend because he was inconsiderate. He'd been a bad boyfriend because as Alonzo, Riccardo and he grew into adulthood and had a right to a share of profits, he'd seen the family finances first strain, then begin to fail. He'd worked his tail off to sell more wine, but he hadn't fixed their money troubles until he got the go-ahead from his dad to sell the family wines online. And he would continue to work his tail off to make sure the family would never have to worry about money again.

All this time, he'd been thinking he would be the one to break up with Lila if they got involved. But Lila was a hundred times smarter than Julia. She'd figure out he wasn't a good bet as a boyfriend the first time he put work ahead of her. He would always put work ahead of everything because no one else in his family did.

Then *he'd* be dumped.

Again.

Because he'd deserve it.

Julia caught Lila's hand. "Boys," she said, looking first at Alonzo, then at Mitch. "You're going to have to excuse me and Lila. There are a few people I'd like her to meet."

Mired in his own confusion, Mitch absently said, "Sure. I'll wait here with Mom and Nanna."

"Great." Julia slid her hand beneath Lila's elbow to guide her away. "You look lovely, Lila."

Mitch's brow furrowed. It was rare for Julia to give a compliment. Though another person might have thought it was nice that she had, Mitch knew it wasn't. The urge to drag Lila away from Julia roared through him, but they were already walking across the grassy lawn.

"Isn't that last year's gown?"

And there it was. That compliment Julia had given Lila had only been a way to get her guard down so she could insult her.

The very second before he would have raced across the yard to rescue her, Lila laughed. "You actually care about those things?" She batted a hand. "I don't have time." She glanced down at her pretty yellow dress. "Besides, beauty is beauty." She smoothed her hand down her skirt. "I think it's a sign of someone who doesn't really have her own style when a woman likes something based on a calendar year or a designer." She smiled at Julia. "Don't you?"

Julia's mouth opened, then closed, then opened again. For once she had absolutely no comeback.

Smothering a laugh behind a fake cough, Mitch glanced at Nanna, who winked.

His bad feelings about Julia's motives morphed into warmth of approval for Lila. She was so much more than he would have ever guessed she was.

Still, being with Julia might bring out the best in Lila, but hugging Julia had not brought out the best in him. It had reminded him of what a bad boyfriend he was, right after Lila had told him he was a demanding boss. But he also suddenly saw what had been right in front of him all along. He didn't have a choice. Though everyone in his family worked, it seemed no one but him knew how to make money. And they needed money. Lots and lots of money to keep up the lifestyle to which they'd become accustomed.

That meant no getting involved with Lila. If he wanted to keep her as an employee—wanted to help her if she was pregnant—he couldn't hurt her. If they took this charade into reality, she'd figure out she came second, and she wouldn't stay on as his assistant. Then he wouldn't be able to help her.

No matter how sassy and strong and really, really fun she was, he had to keep their relationship strictly professional.

Looking at her in the sexy yellow dress, with her sleek hair and her bright smile, he held back a groan. When it came to pretty girls, he was not known for his self-control. Plus, he still had to play the part of loving fiancé—hold her hand, kiss her.

This was not going to be easy.

# CHAPTER SEVEN

LILA NOTICED THE minute Mitch changed. When he'd hugged Julia, the expression on his face had flattened, as if he'd thought of something terrible. He didn't say anything, but he didn't have to. She could read him very well and she had a bad feeling about this. He was finally noticing her— Real Lila—and they were communicating with her being her. Then he'd hugged Julia and gone quiet. He'd shut down. He'd even let Julia sweep her away from him.

He might be attempting to be a good best man, a good Ochoa, who gladly accepted Julia into their clan and didn't mind her spiriting Lila away. But maybe when he'd hugged Julia he'd remembered how much he'd loved her—

No. He'd said a million times that he was over

her. She'd seen him happy. He did not still love Julia.

Then what had caused that horrible expression to come to his face?

Julia walked Lila across the gorgeous yard of her family's home. The stunning view of the mountain backdrop was enhanced by rows and rows of grapes. A warm sun beat down. Smooth, sweet air enveloped them.

As they headed toward a grove of trees, Julia said, "So how did you meet Mitcham... Oh, wait, that's right. You're his assistant."

Lila smiled, wishing they'd get to the people Julia wanted her to meet so she could go back to Mitch and figure out what was going on with him. "Yes. We work together."

"Long nights together caused you to talk?"

That certainly wasn't a lie. Though they'd been discussing work, they'd still talked. "Yes."

Julia stopped walking and pressed her fingers onto Lila's forearm. "Come on," she cajoled. "No one's really heard details, and I for one am curious."

She supposed she should have expected this. The former girlfriend wanted the scoop. She'd seen the way Julia gazed at Alonzo. She didn't have feelings for Mitch. She was just snooping for some juicy gossip.

"Don't be curious," she said with a laugh. "We're sort of boring."

When Julia smiled triumphantly, Lila's heart thumped. That wasn't the expression of a woman looking for gossip. It was the victorious glow of someone who'd caught her in a lie. As a woman who'd dated Mitch, Julia would know time spent with him would never be boring. Lila's flip answer had just taken the first step to ruining the charade.

Thinking quickly, she added, "If going to restaurant openings, clubs and New York's wonderful theaters are to be considered boring."

Julia frowned. "Oh. So you were…teasing me?"

Relief skittered through Lila. She took a second to compose herself before she said, "Not teasing. Making a joke. Of course our courtship is exciting. We live in the most wonderful city in the world." Even though she knew she was digging her and Mitch into a pit, one she'd have to explain to him so he could confirm everything she said, she realized it was necessary. If Julia was poking around to find something wrong in Mitch's engagement, they would have to step up their game.

Julia took her arm again and led her in the direction of a gaggle of women clustered by the trees. She introduced them as her bridesmaids. Lila happily said hello, accepted congratulations on her engagement and then excused herself.

Because there was no reason for Lila to meet the bridesmaids, it was abundantly clear Julia had used that excuse to get a private minute with her. She was definitely looking for a crack in their relationship. She had to talk to Mitch. Now.

But the conversation at Nanna's table was bright and lively as most of the party guests came over to greet Nanna. There was never an opening for her to ask Mitch to walk around the grounds with her so she could tell him about Julia. When Julia's parents offered a congratulatory toast for Julia and Alonzo, Lila tried leaning into Mitch to make it look like she was love struck, in case Julia was watching, but it was as if he didn't notice. He didn't put his arm around her, pull her close or even talk to her. Later, when Alonzo and Julia came over to chat with the people at the table next to Nanna's, Lila tried holding Mitch's hand, but he slid it away to use it to make a point.

And she clearly saw what Julia saw. Two people who really weren't in love. She had no idea why Julia thought she had to expose them, but if they didn't fix this, Lila had no doubt that she would.

It was almost the end of the evening before she could lure Mitch away from the table. She deliberately led him to an empty spot under two huge shade trees. Glancing around to make sure there was no one near enough to overhear, she whispered, "Julia is onto us."

He laughed. "Are you kidding? You've been handling her beautifully. I think we're fine."

"We are not fine," Lila began. The last thing she expected was that he wouldn't believe her. How could she explain that he never looked at her with love in his eyes? Or touched her automatically?

Or, worse, that he'd pulled his hand out of hers when she tried to make the charade look realistic?

The only thing she could think to say was, "It wasn't merely what she said. It was the way she used a weird excuse to get me alone, as if she was angling for a chance to find something wrong."

"Did you ever stop to think that that's because she doesn't like you?"

Lila gaped at him. "If that's true, then you're making my point. She's watching us. We need to make this engagement more believable."

Mitch awkwardly stepped closer. "Okay."

Lila's heart jumped to her throat. His awkwardness made things worse.

But her nervousness about being so near didn't help either. Cuddling up to each other was exactly what they needed to do—look like two people in love, stealing a private moment. Except after this past twenty-four hours of ditching her persona and being only Real Lila, it wasn't quite so easy to be Lila, Fake Fiancée. Especially not when she wanted this to be her moment, her chance to get him to like *her*. But he was awkward. As if he'd forgotten he'd kissed her—for real—the night before.

She resisted the urge to shake her head. He could not have forgotten that kiss. The man was interested.

She gingerly put her hands on his lapels. Regardless of what Julia said, Lila loved this man. And he had begun to more than notice her. There were a million reasons he could be nervous now. A million reasons he could have gotten a weird expression on his face when he hugged Julia. Including the fact that he might not like her. The woman *had* betrayed him.

"If we were really engaged, you'd probably look more comfortable doing that."

She wasn't surprised it was easier to touch him when she knew it wasn't real. Fake Lila could do any darned thing she wanted with no consequence. Real Lila knew how much was riding on this. She *wanted* to flatten her hands on his chest. To run them up to his collar so she could ease her fingers through the hair at his nape. Then she could easily pull his head down for a kiss.

*That's* what she'd do if they were really engaged. That's what she'd wanted to do since the day she'd met him.

*That's* what she would do now.

She eased her palms along the smooth material of his jacket, enjoying the decadent richness of the fabric, but it still didn't feel right. And she finally understood why. She was trying to take this relationship into reality because she could see he was getting feelings for her—but he didn't know her. She'd already realized that until she told him the truth about her life, her childhood, he couldn't really fall in love with *her*. She didn't know why she was trying to seduce him now, without telling him.

She sucked in a breath, pulling her hands away. "There is something important I should tell you about me."

His face changed. The fun-loving expression left and was replaced by a look that somehow combined seriousness and expectancy. He put his hands on her shoulders supportively. "I think I know what it is."

That was the last thing she expected him to say. It confused her so much she said, "You do?"

He stiffened. "Yes. You're pregnant."

She had no idea there were levels of shock, but her head jangled with something so incomprehensible she might have created a new one.

"What? No! I'm not pregnant!" All thoughts of her mother and the horrible childhood she'd brought on herself fled. She swatted his upper arm. "What's wrong with you? Why the hell would you think that?"

"When you said you didn't drink, Nanna sort of jumped to conclusions."

She gaped at him. "Nanna thought I was *pregnant* because I don't drink?"

"Well, that and because she said you had a certain glow."

If she had "a certain glow" it was because she was thrilled to be at his home, *with him*, just plain spending time with him.

She pulled her hands away from his and dropped her head into her palms. "Does your whole family think that?"

"No. Just Nanna."

She glanced up sharply. "And you?"

He shook his head. "I didn't know what to think."

"But you weren't sure?"

"Well, you never tell me anything."

And now she knew why. Real Lila absolutely, positively didn't fit into his world. She was awkward and simple. She wouldn't in a million years have thought his family would assume she was pregnant because she didn't drink. She wasn't a sophisticated thinker. She'd been foolish to even consider she belonged here. She had no place with these people.

And she was done embarrassing herself. She most certainly wouldn't tell him the truth about her life now. From here on out, she would only be Fake Lila.

Spotting Riccardo walking toward them, Lila nudged her head to the right so Mitch would look over and see him.

As he got closer, Mitch said, "Hey, what's up?"

Riccardo didn't reply until he was almost on

top of them, then he lowered his voice. "I had a conversation with Julia tonight. I'm pretty sure she's onto you."

Glad to be thinking of anything other than how Mitch's family thought she was pregnant, she shifted back into her role as his coconspirator. "I told you."

"*Sí*. You did." He caught her gaze, his eyes filled with remorse, but he turned to face Riccardo. "So what do we do?"

"You're going to have to start looking a little more like two people who want to get married."

Mitch's gaze crawled back to hers. She swore he was silently seeking forgiveness for thinking she was pregnant. But she was the one who was sorry. If she hadn't wanted a real shot with him and hadn't considered telling him the truth about herself, none of this awkwardness would have happened.

Including the fact that Julia wouldn't be onto them. Fake Lila was a much better fiancée choice for Mitch than Real Lila.

Riccardo said, "If it somehow gets out that your

engagement is fake, this charade won't have saved your butt. It will have made matters worse."

Mitch sighed. "No kidding. Lila and I need to go back to the apartment and regroup. Luckily, the show's over for tonight." He glanced around. "Half the guests have gone home." He held out his hand to her. "Come on. Let's say good-night to our hosts, get the limo and go."

She took his hand, brightened her smile, leaned into his arm.

Fake Lila was alive and well and ready to take over. And Real Lila wasn't coming out again—at all—unless she was alone in her bedroom. Because of trying to be herself, she'd almost ruined this whole damned charade.

They found Julia and Alonzo. Alonzo kissed Lila's cheek, while Mitch kissed Julia's cheek.

"Thank you for coming."

Lila smiled fondly at Julia. "Thank you for having us. It was a lovely party. Your parents have a beautiful home." Then she gazed lovingly at Mitch, snuggled into his arm. "I'm ready to go when you are."

Mitch shook Alonzo's hand. He said, "We'll see you tomorrow," and they walked around to the front of the house to the limo.

The moon had risen to a glorious height and cast a heavenly glow on everything. Even the grapevines gleamed surreally, and Lila realized it was all so perfect, so beautiful that she should have immediately recognized she didn't belong in this place with this family. From here on out, every time she looked at the perfection around her, every time she slid into a limo, or put on clothes she couldn't afford in her real life, it would fortify her resolve to stay in character and protect herself.

# CHAPTER EIGHT

MITCH HELPED HER into the back seat of the limo, then climbed in behind her. She'd thrown him for a loop when she'd said she had to tell him something about herself. It was clearly so difficult for her that he'd tried to save her some agony and incorrectly guessed she was pregnant. But that didn't mean the conversation was over. He needed to know her problem, her secret, so he could figure out how to keep her in his employ and how he could help her. Now that he had his head on straight about not getting involved with her, it would be much easier.

"Let's go back to talking about what we were talking about before Riccardo came over."

She smoothed the skirt of her pretty yellow dress. "It's not important."

"Really? Because the very serious look on your

face told me that it was. Plus, you said it was something you had to tell me."

She laughed and batted a hand. Her fake fiancée persona fully in place, she casually said, "I was just going to say I should tell you a couple of stories about my roommates that would help us to continue to be more familiar with each other so there'll be no more slipups."

His heart twisted a bit. He'd embarrassed her so much by asking if she was pregnant that she wasn't going to tell him. No matter how much he pushed. In fact, pushing might be the worst thing to do. Which meant the best thing to do would be to back off until he found another time to bring it up. Maybe after a day or two she'd get comfortable with him again and be able to open up.

Tabling the conversation for the moment, he relaxed on the limo seat. "Okay. Have at it."

She started with a story about one of her roommates illegally keeping a cat in her room that made him laugh. Then she moved on to a story about pooling their money once a week to get one order of Chinese takeout that they split, and he felt like an idiot.

"Why didn't you ever tell me that you needed more money?"

"Because I checked around. My salary is average for what I do for you. If I want more money, I need to be doing more important things. Things I know how to do. But you don't need."

He thought about that. "Is that why you want another job? To get to do those more important tasks?"

"Yes." She glanced down at her dress again.

That was something she did when what she said was difficult for her—or when she was telling him only half the truth. His heart softened again. "You want your job to be challenging?"

She peered over at him. "Who doesn't?"

There was more. He knew there was more, but he could also see she wasn't going to spill it. If he really wanted to help her, he had to work with what he had. "Riccardo and I could probably create a new job for you. Something that wouldn't just be more challenging, it would also pay enough that you could get your own apartment."

She shook her head. "If you'd created a new job on your own because you needed someone, that would have been great. Doing it now, it would feel like charity."

Frustration rose in him and he sat up. "You want a more challenging job that could pay more. Riccardo and I could probably make one for you, but you won't take it because it would be charity?"

"Wouldn't it?"

"No! It would be more or less like you making us aware of a need and us filling it."

"The need is mine. Otherwise you would have already created the job."

"Your circular logic is going to explode my brain one of these days."

She laughed. "Aren't you glad we never talked before this?"

"No. I'm thinking that if we'd talked before this I'd have been more ready."

"You have to take the heat for that one."

That made his eyes narrow. "Why me? Why not you? Why couldn't you have come into the office and said, 'Hey, Mitch, how was your weekend?'"

"I did."

That surprised him. "You did?"

"Every Monday morning for a year. You'd always answer 'fine' without looking up from whatever you were reading."

"Yeah, well, every Monday morning, we also get weekend sales reports. So I was preoccupied."

"So you take the blame."

He put his fingers on his temples to stop the throbbing that had begun there. Luckily, the lane for Ochoa Vineyards came into view.

They got out of the limo, stepping onto the grounds for his family home where anyone could be milling about, meaning the conversation was over until they got behind the closed doors of his apartment. They climbed the steps. He unlocked the door and they walked into the sitting room.

He stopped.

He'd kissed her here the night before. She'd told him that she wanted to think things through, that she wasn't ready, and tonight she'd probably been about to tell him why and he'd blown it by asking her if she was pregnant.

She headed directly to her room, but she paused. Facing him, she politely said, "Good night."

But she didn't wait for him to return her goodnight. She all but raced to the open door and scurried to get herself behind it.

Shrugging out of his jacket, he strode toward his bedroom. The weirdest sensation enveloped him. Something like a pounding need. She'd been two seconds away from telling him something very serious and very important, and trying to help her, he'd rushed in, making a guess that was wrong. His usual arrogance had cost him a chance, but by God he was not letting this drop. No matter what hoop he had to jump through, she would tell him.

"How were your meetings today?"

Lila stepped out of her bedroom talking. Because of more Ochoa Wines business, she hadn't seen Mitch all day and had enjoyed an afternoon by the pool with Nanna, who was incredibly apologetic for thinking Lila was pregnant.

Mitch's grandmother was also hosting a private family dinner that night. Careful now that Julia was clearly watching them, Lila had once again asked Nanna what she should wear, and Nanna had suggested a flirty floral skirt and white tank top because the evening was supposed to be casual. Family being family. Not socializing.

Resigned to going back to being Fake Lila and fairly pleased with the way she looked in the happy skirt, she smiled at Mitch. "I almost felt guilty sitting by the pool for hours knowing you were working."

He walked to the apartment door. "Don't. It's good for you to keep Nanna company. Besides, I love my job."

Something about the way he said that struck her oddly. He opened the door for her and she stepped out into the small hallway.

"I know you love your job."

He motioned for her to go down the stairs. "I *created* my job. I searched around, looking for something I loved, something that made me as much money as I wanted, and I didn't stop until I found it."

Walking down the steps, she frowned. She hadn't missed the way he'd emphasized the word *created*. Obviously, he wasn't going to drop last night's conversation, but that didn't mean she had to take the bait. "Well, you did great figuring it all out."

At the bottom of the steps, he stopped her before she reached the door. "*Sí.* I did. And I don't ever pretend that I'm not proud of myself."

Still not taking the bait. "You should be."

"So last night I also realized that that thing you almost told me yesterday—when I stupidly asked you if you were pregnant—is probably part of the reason you won't let me create a job for you."

Wow. He might be a little slower than Nanna, but he was pretty damned perceptive too. Still, she'd hit this wall the night before. She was not in the same league as these people. No matter how much she liked Mitch, she wasn't the right girl for him. Pretending she was or might be or could be would only make a fool of her. So no matter how much he pushed or hinted, she would keep her secrets to herself.

"Seriously, it was nothing. And it's not related to our pretending to be engaged."

He studied her for an agonizing twenty seconds. Twenty seconds that had never felt so long. She knew he didn't give up on anything, but maybe he hadn't ever been in a tug-of-war with a person who'd basically been taking care of herself since she was four. Because there was no way in hell she was telling him about her past. After the mistake she made with her mom, she could keep a secret, hold her tongue, pretend everything was fine better than anyone. Particularly after how he'd reacted last night. Raised in a mansion with tons of money and even more love, Mitch had no idea how her side of the world ran.

When she'd had her raging crush on him, she'd always envisioned that when she told him about her past, he would be sympathetic. She'd pictured him telling her she was brave for wanting to find her mom and make up for the blunder she'd made at ten. But when she'd thought it through the night before—ensconced in the bedroom that spoke of the wealth of his world, the privilege, the love that he and his family took for granted—she suddenly realized he wouldn't see it that way. What would a man who adored his parents think if he knew she was the one who'd called Child Services on her mom? She'd been a little girl, a cold, hungry little girl. Her only food was the free lunch she got at school on weekdays. She'd spent most of her first ten years alone and scared.

So she'd forgiven herself for taking the step she naively thought would solve her problems. But what would Mitch think? For her to have been taken away from her mom, he had to know her childhood hadn't been good. But he didn't know the extent of it. How could a guy who'd grown up with such perfection understand such poverty? Such pain? Not just her own but her mom's?

He wouldn't.

So she wouldn't tell him.

"You're sure it's nothing? Because we still have an entire week of this charade. You and Riccardo both think Julia's onto us. We can't afford to have any slipups."

She nodded. "I'm perfectly capable of keeping up the charade until we go back to New York."

He said, "Good," and the expression in his eyes said he believed her, but he continued to search her gaze.

She stared into his dark, dark eyes, holding her ground, almost daring him to push for more, knowing he didn't have another angle into the conversation about her job or her secret, and she'd satisfactorily handled the one in he'd had.

Finally, he looked away. He caught her hand and turned toward the door, but he stopped again. "If this thing falls apart, it's going to be more than embarrassing. It will look like I had something to hide or a reason to go to the extreme of pretending to be engaged."

"You did. You were trying to keep the focus of this wedding on your brother."

"True."

"But we're not going to fail."

He opened the door and she stepped out into the soothing evening sun.

They were quiet for a few seconds, then he casually said, "You're so sure of yourself."

She laughed. Sure of herself was the last term she'd use. What she was was protective.

"No. I'm sure of you. You don't lose, Mitcham Ochoa. I've been watching you win for an entire year. If I have confidence, it's in you."

He sniffed a laugh. "Right."

"It is right. You're a winner. You're one of those people who just has to crook his little finger and things fall into place."

He frowned. "That's how you see me?"

"Isn't that the way your life is?"

"I lost my girlfriend to my brother. That same brother will inherit the top position for the vineyard. I looked around when I was twenty-four and realized I would be a footnote in Alonzo's tenure as vintner for Ochoa Wines if I didn't figure something out."

She shrugged. "And you did."

He sighed. "*Sí.* I did."

"I would think you would be a little more proud of that."

"I am proud. Very proud." He sucked in a breath. "Ochoa Online pulled the vineyard out of the jaws of bankruptcy."

They were only a few feet away from the main house, so she almost stopped walking. But the grounds were unusually quiet, and she suspected that's why Mitch spoke openly. So she did too.

"I thought Ochoa Vineyards was very successful?"

"It was, but we weren't selling enough wine to keep three families. My dad couldn't see the potential of e-commerce, but I wanted a shot at selling wine online and when I got it, I made it work."

"See. There you go. Back to being a winner."

"In everyone's eyes but my family's."

She frowned at him, totally confused, and he laughed. "I don't want to sound like I need credit for what I did. I just want you to see that sometimes success is in the eyes of the beholder. You look at me as if you think I was born under a lucky star, and in some ways, I was. But my life is far from perfect and a person doesn't just fall into the category of winner. Most of us work for it."

She knew all that, of course. When she compared her life to his, he did look like a guy who had it fairly easy. But she lived the truth. She was with him every day at his office. "I know how hard you work. I'm sorry."

"It's okay. Truth be told, I liked saving my family."

She laughed. "You're such a guy."

He chuckled and shifted his grip on her hand. "I know. There's a lot of male pride in a Spanish family."

"No kidding."

"So you can see why I didn't want my dad connecting Julia dumping me to the work I did with Ochoa Online. I virtually saved my family. I found a position of authority for me and Riccardo in a situation where we might not have had one. I don't want people saying I only did that because Julia dumped me, when exactly the opposite is true. Julia dumped me because I was too

busy for her. And what I was busy doing was figuring out how to sell more wine so that we could
all continue to live like kings."

"You think she dumped you because you were
too busy?"

He sighed. "If you look at this from her vantage
point, I wasn't a good boyfriend. I wasn't around.
I was always traveling, searching for new ways
to sell wines because my dad wouldn't give me
permission to build a website. In her eyes, she
shifted to a man who paid attention to her."

"Wow."

"For a good five years, I had known the family
was headed for trouble financially. But it wasn't
until she dumped me that I got permission to do
the one thing that would save us."

"And this," she said, waving her engagement
ring at him, "is sort of your way of distancing
yourself from Julia so your family doesn't feel
sorry for you. They see what you did?"

He shrugged. "I really do want Alonzo and Julia's wedding to be theirs. But I also wish my fam-

ily could separate our breakup and the creation of Ochoa Online."

"So let's get in there and make them believe we're the happiest couple on the face of the earth."

He laughed and opened the door to the vineyard's main house. They hurried up the stairs and back down the hall to Nanna's quarters.

As they stepped into the living room where everyone was enjoying a cocktail, Lila watched Julia's expression shift and confirmed—again—that Julia was suspicious.

But for once, she didn't care. Not only was Julia a jittery bride, looking for trouble, but also the two-minute conversation they'd had walking to the house had infused her with new energy for the ruse.

It had also given her the weirdest feeling about Mitch. She'd only seen his successes—and, yes, there were many. But she never considered that his family expected this of him and that it would bother him that they didn't seem to appreciate the wonderful things he had done.

Dressed in simple pink trousers and a white

top, Marguerite walked over. She handed Mitch a glass of wine and Lila a glass of club soda before she kissed both of their cheeks. "I'm glad Nanna wanted dinner to be informal. It's good to relax after a day of meetings."

Mitch laughed. "Except some people sat by the pool while we worked."

"Yes, we did," Nanna chimed in, totally un-apologetic. Wearing white capris and a navy-blue-and-white-striped T-shirt, she looked casual and comfortable, like a woman about to go out for a sail.

Mitch directed Lila to the gray sofa and as she sat, Mitch's father, Santiago, said, "So, Lila, you and I have barely said two words to each other. Are you enjoying your stay here?"

Surprised to have Mitch's father pay attention to her, she said, "I'm enjoying my stay very much. Your vineyard is beautiful. And Nanna's pretty good company."

Everybody laughed.

Julia said, "She's just glad to have someone to hang out with."

Nanna shook her head. "No. I *choose* to be alone sometimes." She reached out and squeezed Lila's hand. "I only give up my privacy for special people."

Her eyes shining, Marguerite said, "We could start talking about your wedding while you're here."

Knowing this was exactly the opposite of what Mitch wanted, she said, "We just got engaged. I haven't really thought much about it. Besides, this is Julia and Alonzo's special time."

Julia shrugged. "I have no problem talking about your wedding. In fact, I'm curious."

Of course she was. This was one of those moments Lila had to make sure everything between her and Mitch looked real.

Lila glanced at Mitch, who smiled as if to say, "Go ahead. Say what you want."

She faced Marguerite again. "I think having the wedding here would be wonderful."

Santiago grinned. "Really?"

Marguerite clapped her hands together. "I was

so afraid you'd say you want to be married in the States."

"No. It's beautiful here. Perfect."

Mitch said, "Yes, it's perfect here." He took Lila's hand and kissed the knuckles. The intimacy of his lips touching her skin filled her with warmth. Mostly because, like the kiss in the kitchen, it felt real. Tonight he'd shared something with her that his assistant Lila never in a million years would have gotten the chance to know. Her heart expanded almost to overflowing. It was the first time he'd ever been so honest, so normal with her. If nothing else, they were becoming friends.

So... Yeah. The touch of his lips on her skin felt different.

Genuine.

Then he shifted the discussion in the direction of tuxes and Alonzo's bachelor party. And she watched him as he talked. It was clear he loved his family and she could understand his pride at saving Ochoa Vineyards. She glanced at Julia, thought of her not as annoying but the first woman who had loved Mitch. She studied his mom, his dad, Nanna and even Riccardo and his parents and realized it probably wasn't easy to keep ten people happy. Yet Mitch did it. Every darned day. Day in and day out. And he did it without any credit. His brother ran the vineyard. His dad ran the business. And Mitch was the one who actually made them money by selling the wines. Mitch would always be second to his brother—who was second to their dad.

Of all the people in this room, Mitch was probably the smartest, and craftiest, yet you'd never know it from how he behaved. He deferred to his dad, loved his brother, doted on his nanna and his mom.

And somehow it made him all the sexier.

The staff announced dinner. Mitch's dad waited for her as they all walked into the dining room. Taking her hand, Santiago slid it onto his forearm as he escorted her to the table. "So you like it here? You like Spain?"

Temporarily shelving her thoughts about Mitch, Lila smiled at him. "I love it here."

He walked her to her seat and pulled out her

chair. In her peripheral vision she saw Mitch scramble to get his mom's chair. She also saw his eyes narrow as his dad said, "We have incredible weather year-round."

Marguerite said, "The best."

Mitch walked to the seat beside Lila. "We'll have to visit later in the year so Lila can see for herself."

"That would be wonderful," Santiago said. Facing Lila, he added, "And you can bring your family."

"Oh." She glanced at Mitch, then at Riccardo, whose eyebrows were raised the whole way to his hairline. She wasn't sure if his panicked expression meant he'd told somebody she'd grown up in foster care, or if his panicked expression meant he hadn't. But that was the problem. If she said, "Sure, that'll be great. I'm sure my family would love to meet you all," somebody at this table could say, "I thought you were a foster kid."

Actually, Nanna could say that. The first day she was here she'd told Nanna she'd been raised in foster homes.

She had to stick with the truth.

She glanced back at Santiago. "I'm sorry. I just assumed Mitch would have told you that I was raised in foster care."

Marguerite said, "Oh, no! You have no family? No one to invite to the wedding?"

A quick glance around the table showed eight very sad faces. Except for Nanna, who gave her a smile of encouragement.

"It wasn't as bad as everybody thinks it is." She peeked up at Mitch, who studied her intently, as if hoping she'd finally fill in some of the blanks for him. Her heart somersaulted in her chest. After the way he'd been so honest with her on the walk over, she almost felt she could. Or maybe she *should*. But this wasn't the time or place. "Plus, I have a lot of friends."

Obviously eager to get beyond his faux pas, Santiago boisterously said, "That's wonderful! You can invite them all. You and Mitch will have a big, happy wedding."

Lila said, "That'd be great," satisfied that she'd smoothed over that potential bad spot. But a tiny bit of guilt suddenly pinched her chest. She wanted to tell Mitch the truth about her life. So why hadn't she corrected the Ochoas when they assumed she had no family? She might not have brothers and sisters or a dad, but her mom was still alive. It would have been an easy way to open the door to have the discussion about her past when they returned to the apartment.

So why hadn't she?

She shook her head to clear it.

*It didn't matter. This was a ruse. Not real.*

If she were getting married for real she would want her mom there. She would move heaven and earth to find her. There was no reason for her to feel as if she'd somehow disrespected her mom by not mentioning her.

But she still felt guilty. Wrong.

She'd dealt her mother the ultimate insult when she'd called Child Services and gotten herself placed in foster care. Now she was pretending she didn't exist—

Before she could finish that thought, another,

stronger truth ruffled through her, like the first blast of wind from an oncoming storm.

The two times she'd finagled enough money to locate her mom, her mom had taken off. Disappeared as if she'd never existed.

What if she didn't want to be found?

What if she didn't want Lila in her life?

What if that was the real fear Lila had always had but couldn't admit because it was just too horrible to contemplate?

And what if that was why she'd created the big fairy-tale crush around Mitch as soon as she'd started working for him? The past year, she'd been quietly content, thinking she was staying with Mitch, hoping he'd pay attention to her. Her crush had kept her from looking for a job that paid more, so she'd have money to search for her mom, but most of all it had kept her from admitting the brutal truth...

That her mom didn't want her.

# CHAPTER NINE

MITCH GLANCED OVER at Lila. Her face had gone white. She didn't look like she was even breathing. Talk of her foster care experience had all but paralyzed her.

They made it through dinner because the conversation shifted away from them and over to Julia, but the walk back to his apartment was made in complete silence. A slow ache built in his chest. He knew if she'd just talk about this, he could somehow make it better. He always could.

In the apartment entryway, he said, "I told you my biggest secret on the way over. And you repay me with silence?"

She started up the stairs. "Your dad suggesting I invite my family sort of threw me for a loop."

He followed her. When she didn't elaborate, he said, "I thought we'd made a connection. You know—"

She reached the apartment door and waited for him to catch up with her.

Pulling out his key, he added, "I'd tell you something about me. You'd tell me something about you."

"Is that why you told me about the bankruptcy? And you saving them? So I'd talk?"

He opened the door. "No. I did that so you would understand the importance of our mission being successful. I might not be the one who gets credit for being the leader but I am the leader in this family. I'm the one making the money that holds us together. I cannot be perceived as weak."

She turned to him with one of her fake smiles. "I get it. I do. And we will be successful." Without waiting for his reply, she headed for her bedroom.

She didn't say good-night.

Every other night, no matter how confused or angry, she'd always said good-night.

The strangest urge to follow her raced through him. He wanted to grab her arm and stop her from walking away. Not because he was angry that she wouldn't talk. But because it broke his heart that there was something that made her unbearably sad. He wanted to tell her that whatever was wrong, he would fix it. It was what he did. His brother loved his girlfriend; he stepped aside. Ochoa Vineyards was in trouble; he created Ochoa Online. *He fixed things.*

But he couldn't fix whatever was wrong in Lila's life if she didn't tell him.

The next morning, she came out of her room dressed in jeans and a shirt. As she walked to the kitchen table, she said, "Nanna called. She said you guys have some sort of vintners meeting?"

Her comments were offhand, almost light, but when he looked into her kitten-gray eyes he saw the sadness she couldn't quite cover up.

"Yes. My dad hopes to drum up a little more business for the website that sells wines for other vineyards. He's invited them here so he can tell them about Ochoa Online and see if we can get their wines on the multi-producer site."

Her head tilted. "But that's your company.

Ochoa Vineyards is a client of Ochoa Online. *You* own Ochoa Online."

"My dad still sees it all being under the same umbrella. Besides, he's helping me." He rose from his seat. She looked tired and worn, as if she hadn't slept the night before. "Can I get you some coffee?"

She waved him off. "I'll get it."

He lowered himself to his chair, feeling weird again. She'd been perfectly fine. Feisty even. Until his dad mentioned her family the night before, and she'd had to admit she'd been in foster care. Now her face was drawn. Her usually warm gray eyes had dimmed.

He couldn't stand to see her this way. But he also didn't know what it was about being a foster child that tore her up. He knew the basics of her life. To be a foster child, she didn't have any family who could raise her. But she'd been dealing with this her entire life. Why did admitting it to his family make her so sad?

She poured a mug of coffee and walked to the

table with the tray of bagels and pastries the chef had sent up.

Pulling out a chair, she said, "So your dad likes being involved in *your* companies too?"

"My dad's a Spanish man. He's a family man. He believes he has the right to comment on, interfere with and downright run anything that belongs to anyone he loves."

She laughed. "That's funny."

He sat back in his seat, glad her mood seemed to be improving. "It's not so funny if you're the one running the business he's interfering in."

"He can't interfere a lot. I'm your assistant. I'm in the office every time you are, and I've never seen him do anything."

"That's because nothing he's suggested has ever made it to our idea meetings. He makes phone calls. Suggests shifts. Gives ideas. And Riccardo and I listen, but don't take action on anything he says."

"Sounds like he's just being a good dad."

He shook his head. "Lila, I'm thirty. I don't want my daddy telling me what to do."

She laughed again and his heart lifted, but they'd sort of run out of conversation. Unless they were talking about the ruse or his family or Ochoa Online, she didn't really talk to him.

Something had made her sad. She wanted to leave his employ and he was powerless to help her. He had never had this feeling of helplessness before.

He rose from his seat. "I guess I'd better run."

She nodded. "Yes, Nanna will be around for me soon."

He stood by the table, not quite wanting to leave, too awkward to stay. The urge to press her for answers shimmered through him, but in over a week he hadn't been able to get her to talk to him. Last night she'd totally shut down. Maybe it was time to admit defeat?

"Enjoy your day."

She smiled slightly. "I will. Nanna's always fun."

"Spend money."

She laughed. "Oh, I'll do that too."

He finally turned and walked to the door, a strange thought weaving through his brain. Her laughter had been real, and he liked hearing her laugh, making her laugh, almost as much as he'd liked sharing a confidence with her.

He knew she'd had a hard life. Now he knew that working for him hadn't been the joy he'd always thought it was. Being in Spain, with his family, was fun for her. So maybe instead of trying to get her to tell him her secrets, what he should be doing was making sure every step of this charade was fun for her.

Wednesday night, the second welcome ball began almost the same way the first had. Lila came out of her bedroom in a cobalt-blue satin gown, looking good enough to eat. Mitch adjusted the cuffs on his white shirt before sliding into his tuxedo jacket.

"You look amazing."

She smiled. "Thank you."

He motioned to the door and Lila preceded him out of the apartment and down the stairs.

They hadn't had a chance to have another private conversation since the one on Monday morning. Still, he'd accepted that she wasn't going to talk, and he had a new plan. Julia could be the crowned princess of the world that night, and hog up all the family attention to her heart's delight, because he was a man on a mission. He was going to make sure Lila enjoyed this evening.

They walked out into the warm night air and she looked up and sighed. "Oh, my gosh! Look at those stars."

He peeked at her. "You've seen stars before."

"Not like this. Not in the city."

He took her hand. The gesture had become as natural, as easy as breathing. "Don't you get out of the city much?"

"I've never been out of the city. I mean, except now. Being here is my first time away from New York."

That shocked him, then he wondered why. Her life was compact, filled with purpose. She had to work to support herself. Work was the key to everything for her. His life was filled with purpose, too, and he also believed work was the key to fulfilling his responsibilities. But he had releases, options that she didn't have. Tonight he would make up for that.

"Then I'm glad I'm with you when you see the stars."

She stopped walking. It looked as if she was going to say something, but she shook her head as if to clear it and started walking again. Disappointment rattled through him, but he was growing accustomed to that now.

When they stepped onto the sidewalk that led to the back entry to the main house and the corridor that would take them to the ballroom, she did the thing where she pressed herself up against his arm and disappointment turned to disgust.

At first when she'd cuddled against him, he'd realized she was trying to give people the impression they were close. Now that he was getting to know her and now that they'd held hands and even kissed for real once, it felt fake to him. Really fake. So fake he wondered if that wasn't the thing that made Julia suspicious about their relationship.

"What are you doing?"

She gazed up at him.

Confusion flickered through him. That adoring expression wasn't "her" either.

With other guests milling about the grounds, he couldn't say anything. But the looks of adoration she gave him as they wove through the crowded ballroom, saying hello, and through dinner only frustrated him. She'd been doing this all along and it had seemed perfect. But tonight it set his nerve endings on edge.

He didn't want to entertain *this* woman. He didn't want to dance with *this* woman.

He wanted to entertain Lila. His assistant. He wanted to make her laugh. He wanted to make her forget whatever problem she had. He wanted *her* to have some fun.

As dinner concluded and the lights on the dance floor dimmed and the lights on the stage lit, Lila struggled to keep her smile in place. For the past two days, she'd managed to avoid Nanna and stay away from Mitch, spending most of the time in bed.

The pain of admitting she'd secretly suspected her mom didn't want to be in her life pressed down on her. She'd tried to tell herself it wasn't true. That her mother wanted her. Then she asked herself why? Why would her mother want the child who'd turned her in to the authorities?

And she knew there was no reason.

Alonzo and Julia danced the first dance. Both sets of parents joined them for the second song. And Lila knew what was coming. When the music started for the third dance, Mitch rose, and she held out her hand to him, like a good fiancée.

His smile was warm, loving. "Shall we?"

She matched his sweet smile. Though Julia was far away, there were a hundred other guests to fool, and now more than ever she knew the importance of this ruse. Not only had Mitch saved his family but he wanted to be able to continue to do so. Even without credit. Like a strong Spanish man. In some ways, she thought his sentiment outdated. In other ways, she thought it very cool that he could let his brother have all the attention and his dad meddle to his heart's delight.

Her smile for him grew a notch. With everything she learned about Mitch, she liked him a little more. She wanted to help him. "I'd love to dance."

He walked her to the dance floor and pulled her into his arms. Lila smiled up at him adoringly, making sure the ruse was in place, and he paused.

"What do you say we forget about our engagement for one night?"

She hurriedly glanced around to make sure no one was listening. "You want to break up?"

He laughed. "No. I want to be us tonight."

Her brow furrowed. "Us?"

"You. Me. Real us. A few times we've let our guard down and had a lot of fun. I think I'd like to do that tonight."

She tried to answer but her tongue stuck to the roof of her mouth. He'd had fun with her? Not Fake Lila?

The slow dance finished, but the band immediately began playing another tune. A song she'd never heard.

He grinned. "Samba."

"Oh. Bad timing." Or good timing for the Lila

who was on the dance floor totally confused. She understood him wanting to have a good time. If they did that, they'd look like a real couple, enjoying each other's company. But she wasn't in the mood to have real fun. She'd much rather pretend her way through this. "I don't know how to samba."

He caught her hand. "Don't worry. I do. Just follow me. We start with a box step, then when I push back, you step back. I'll twirl you a few times. Then we're back to the box step. Then when I let go of your hand, you just do what I do...turn one way then the other."

She gaped at him. "I once tried a Zumba class and had to quit because I have two left feet."

He laughed. "Come on. It will be fun."

As he pulled her into the typical hold, she noticed everybody was dancing, having fun, and no one was paying any attention to them. She relaxed a bit, especially through the box steps, which were easy.

Then he lifted his hands from her waist and he took both of her hands. He stepped back and she stepped back. He pulled her close again, then nudged her back again.

She laughed. She supposed it was fun. And a lot easier than Zumba since he was guiding her.

He pulled her into the typical dance hold. They did the box step again. Then he twirled her, and laughter bubbled up from a place so deep inside her, she didn't even know it existed.

All right. Samba was a lot of fun.

He twirled her a few more times, then he let go of her hand and he turned in a circle. She followed his lead.

When he pulled her back into the box step she was laughing. He smiled down at her. "Fun. Right?"

"Yes," she admitted reluctantly, worried she'd spend the whole night dancing if he thought he was entertaining her.

"So relax." He caught her hands again and did the step back, step forward, step back thing. He brought her into the hold for the box step, then he twirled her.

Though the dance floor was full of festive dancers, the rest of the world began to disappear.

She was just plain having fun until he pulled her into the box step hold again and said, "You know, you can swing your hips a bit."

She winced. "Swing my hips?"

"Fun, remember? You're in Spain. Let go a bit."

She'd never, ever, ever had anyone tell her to let go a bit, but why not? She was with people who would never see her again. With a boss who was about to find her a new job. No one would remember this.

She relaxed, glanced at the other female dancers, saw that the hip swaying ranged from his mother's conservative swing to Julia's unabashedly sensual sway, and she started off with a sway more like his mother's.

But then the music sort of took her. It wasn't an easy dance, but it was predictable and the notes flowed through her. Her sway shifted from hip movement to something that encompassed her whole body.

And it was really fun.

The music stopped and the band began to play a flamingo. He quickly explained the steps and they began dancing again.

When he pulled her in close, he looked into her eyes and said, "You're a natural."

She laughed. "I've never been a natural at anything."

"How many things have you tried?"

"Not many." Because she was always preoccupied with her mistakes, her failures, her longing for her mother to be in her life.

"So maybe it's good that you're here in Spain."

"Maybe."

"And maybe it's good we let go again, *sí*?"

She smiled. *"Sí."*

This time he laughed. "I will make a Spanish dancer out of you yet."

She pulled out of his hold, raised one hand and danced away from him. "Or maybe I'm such a natural at this that I'll make you look good in front of your friends."

"You've already managed to make me look like a smarter man to Nanna."

"That was easy."

"She likes you."

"I like her."

Suddenly the world felt as if it opened up to her. Without the burden of finding her mother or an unrequited crush on Mitch pressing down on her, she was just herself. Not Real Lila or Fake Lila, just Lila.

They danced until the band took a break, then they walked to the open bar. She watched the bartender pour wine into a beautiful etched glass flute.

"Wine is actually very pretty."

"Agreed. It's why there are lots of pictures on our website."

She smiled at him. The bartender walked over and he ordered a glass of club soda for her and a beer for himself.

They strolled around talking to a few family friends, and though Lila didn't cling to him or hang on to him, she had the sudden impression they were actually more believable than they ever had been as a couple.

The music began again and they danced to everything the band threw at them. At the end of the set, the music slowed and Mitch pulled her into his arms. She couldn't stop the urge to melt against him and close her eyes.

She'd always wondered what life would feel like when she could stop worrying about having her mom in her life. She'd just always thought she'd stop wondering because she would have found her mom and made peace. She'd never once considered the other side of the coin—that she should give up.

But dancing with Mitch, so close they couldn't get a strand of yarn between them, she was very aware of everything she'd given up all the years she'd searched for her mom. She had absolutely no idea what she would do when she got home— how things would change. But being done with her quest suddenly felt right.

When the song was over, he pulled back, studying her face. "You look tired."

"The last three days have been a little trying."

"Let's get something to drink, then walk back to the apartment."

"But the party's not over."

He shrugged. "We're also not the guests of honor or the hosts. Alonzo and Julia are having a blast. My parents love entertaining." He searched her eyes. "And you're tired."

Tears welled in her eyes. Oh, she was tired. So, so tired.

He took her hand. "Come on." They walked to the bar where he ordered a club soda for her. Then he paused before saying, "You know what? I'll have club soda too."

"You don't have to do that."

His head tilted as he looked at her. "What if I want to?"

"You own a winery. If you're not going to have a beer you should have a glass of wine."

"Unless I want water?"

She laughed. "Now what are you up to?"

"Being with you." He turned when the bartender arrived and took the two club sodas.

The strangest feeling bubbled up in her. He was

sharing her experience. Maybe considering what she felt drinking club soda while everyone else drank wine? It was the oddest way anybody had ever connected with her, yet that's what she felt—that they were connecting.

They drank their club soda listening to another samba. When they were done, he set the glasses on the bar, took her hand and led her outside.

But as soon as they were out of the crowd, on the sidewalk, he let go of her hand, loosened his bow tie and sighed. "That feels better."

Nerves flitted through her. "You're really into being yourself tonight."

He chuckled. "Yeah. I am."

"Well, in that case." She stopped and slipped out of the four-inch-heel sandals. When her feet met cool cobblestone, she sighed. "Now *that* feels better."

"So, you are liking being yourself?"

"A hundred percent."

He took the sandals from her, hooking them over the index finger of his left hand. She expected him to catch her hand, if only to keep up the charade. Instead, he strolled along beside her.

Butterflies filled her. For all the times he'd hugged her, kissed her cheek, put his arm across her shoulders, danced with her, held her hand, *this*—not touching her—seemed a hundred times more romantic.

Because he was with her. Not Fake Lila. Not his pretend fiancée. But *her*.

They reached the duplex and he opened the door, but before she stepped inside, he scooped her up. "I'm not letting you walk on that floor, those steps, without shoes."

Held against his chest, with their faces a few inches apart, she tried to think of something to say but nothing came. The feeling of being held against his chest—of being held, being cared for—shot attraction through her. He was so handsome. So smart. So wonderful. And he was growing to like her.

His eyes narrowed. "What? You think I can't make it up the stairs carrying you?"

She was so busy buzzing with attraction that it

had never occurred to her that she might be too heavy to carry up a flight of stairs. Before she could say anything, he laughed and started to run up the steps.

"I don't have a gym membership for nothing." He nodded at the door. "Reach into my jacket pocket and get the keys."

Still a little shell-shocked, she found the keys.

"It's the one with the green tab."

She inserted it into the lock, twisted, and the doorknob turned. With a light shove the door opened.

Inside the apartment, he caught her gaze and whispered, "Maybe it's not a good idea for you to walk across this carpet without shoes."

"We both did it the other night."

He said, "I don't remember."

She knew that he did. That was her first night as Real Lila with him. That was the night she was just about certain he wanted to lure her into his bedroom.

Her heart thumped in her chest. She could demand that he set her down. But right at this moment, with everything in her life gone—every

hope, every wish, every dream—she just didn't
want to be alone anymore.

He dipped his head and brushed his lips across
hers. She tightened her hands around his neck,
shifting in his arms, getting closer.

His mouth lifted, then smoothed across hers
again before his tongue darted out and she opened
for him. Their tongues danced and entwined. Her
heart rate slowed to a crawl. Everything about the
world slimmed down to him and her. And the fact
that this was real.

Actually, the only times he'd kissed her were
when she was herself.

She felt the connection growing. A click of
rightness so very different than the click she'd
felt when she'd gotten her crush on him.

This was real Mitch kissing real Lila.

This was real.

And for as much as she didn't want to be alone
anymore, she also didn't want to be hurt.

Worse, she didn't want to screw things up
with him. She'd ruined her relationship with her
mother. She might have been a child, but she'd

spent a lifetime paying for that mistake. She didn't want to spend a lifetime paying for another.

She pulled away. A lock of his hair had fallen to his forehead. His lips glowed with dew from their kiss. His dark, observant eyes met hers.

"I think you better put me down."

Her voice came out soft and fragile. She knew that was why he instantly heeded her request. When her bare feet met the floor, she almost turned away, but stopped herself and gazed up at him. "If nothing else, I'm going to take some really great memories home with me."

Then she left him standing in the sitting room, the way she had the last time he'd kissed her.

She closed her bedroom door behind her and leaned against it. A night with him might be worth the broken heart she knew would follow. But this wasn't the moment to choose. She wasn't sure when the moment would arrive, but she was fairly certain she'd know it when it came.

## CHAPTER TEN

THE NEXT MORNING Mitch woke Lila with a brisk knock against her door. "Wear something really comfortable today. After our meetings this morning I'm taking you on a tour of the vineyard."

He had absolutely no idea what was happening between the two of them. He only knew that he hadn't had that much fun with a woman in his entire life. And he hadn't even slept with Lila.

And he wouldn't. Oh, sure, they'd been in the preliminary round the night before with that steamy kiss. But something was going on between them. Something special. He wouldn't ruin it by sleeping with her before she was ready. He also didn't think he could sleep with her until he knew why she was so sad.

Part of him wanted to disagree with that strategy. He had no intention of a permanent relationship with anyone. He had a family to support. He also did not make a good boyfriend, which probably meant he'd make a worse husband.

So he couldn't be thinking thoughts of permanency with Lila.

Still...

He didn't want to stop the natural flow of what was happening between them. Sleep together. Not sleep together. It didn't make any difference. What mattered was that everything evolved naturally. Then there'd be no mistakes. There'd be no hurt feelings.

If he had to choose, he wanted her more as a lover than an assistant. But that was another bridge they would cross when they came to it. He would never let her go empty-handed. When whatever they had fell apart, he would make sure she had another job. A better job. He would make sure she wasn't sorry that she had loved him.

Satisfied, he left the apartment, walked up the cobblestone path with a silly smile, attended a dull, dry meeting with Alonzo, who presented a study on grapes, then begged off lunch. In the restaurant, he grabbed the basket of food he'd ordered that morning and headed back to the apartment.

He opened the door but didn't see Lila, so he called, "Are you ready?"

She came out of her room dressed in skinny jeans and a big, sloppy T-shirt, wearing her glasses.

"That's different."

"These are my own clothes." She caught his gaze. "Too casual?"

The tone of her voice told him that for some reason or another wearing her own clothes was important to her. He presented the basket. "We're having a picnic in the grass. I'd say you're just right." He smiled and held out his hand. "Let's go."

She led him down the flight of stairs, the same stairs he'd carried her up the night before. Crazy sensation spiraled through him and he let it. Whatever was happening between them, he liked it. She did too.

Outside, she stopped on the cobblestone path, gaping at the vehicle before her.

He laughed. "That's my ATV. We're going out." He pointed at the vineyards. "Way out. I want you to see the vineyard, the grapes."

She peeked back at him. "The whole deal, huh?"

"*Sí.*" He walked to his all-terrain vehicle and set the picnic basket in the bin in front. "You've worked for a vineyard for a year. I think it's about time you saw it."

He climbed on and patted the seat behind him. "You're here."

She looked a little nervous but that only made him all the more determined. She'd probably felt out of her league this entire trip, yet she'd held her own. She'd tried everything he'd asked of her— including a samba and flamingo. She wouldn't wimp out now.

She climbed on behind him. Though he could have shifted forward, he liked the feeling of her small body nestled against his. She gingerly slid her arms around his waist, and because she was at his back and couldn't see his face, he smiled. He simply loved the way she felt. In his arms.

Wrapped around him. Dancing with him. It didn't matter.

"Shouldn't we have helmets?"

"You are about to take a leisurely drive along some of Spain's most beautiful land. You should just enjoy."

She pulled in an unsteady breath. "Okay."

He started the engine with a quick flick of his wrist and eased them over a short path that took them to a dirt road that led to the vineyards. The movement of the ATV created a cool breeze that billowed through the heat. They passed rows and rows of grapevines. Wanting her to see everything, he took a few detours, winding between the rows, past ponds and along tiers of new plants.

She didn't say a word. He probably wouldn't have been able to hear her over the roar of the engine, but he sensed that she wouldn't speak. She would want to take it all in. If there was one thing he'd realized about his assistant, it was that she was curious. And when it came to Ochoa Vineyards, he was happy to indulge her.

After they had looped around the entire original vineyard, he brought the ATV to a stop beside a grove of trees that had at one time been the boundary marker for the two vineyards that his father and uncle had combined.

He turned off the engine and it took a few seconds for his ears to adjust to the sound of silence. Soaking in the peace and quiet, he gave them all the time they needed before he turned on the seat to face her and found her eyes shining.

"It's pretty, *sí*?"

"*Pretty* doesn't even begin to describe it. It's huge and open." She shook her head as if bemused. "It's fabulous."

He laughed before motioning for her to climb off the ATV. "I don't think anybody's ever called the vineyard fabulous."

"Well, somebody should, because it's remarkable." She didn't make a move to dismount, just looked around as if unable to get her fill. "It's so green."

"What did you expect?"

"I thought I'd see purple." She laughed. "You know. Grapes. Purple."

"Actually, you'd see red—in July and August."

"Your grapes are red?"

"Most of them. Right now everything is green. Sucking up minerals from the soil."

"How very technical of you."

She got off the ATV, still gazing around.

He shifted his weight to the side and hoisted himself off, then grabbed the picnic basket. "We're at the spot that at one time separated the two vineyards." He pointed to the rows of grapes on the other side of the trees. "That's the second half of Ochoa Vineyards. About a half mile away is the house Riccardo's parents live in."

She stared in the direction as if trying to see the house and finally turned to him. "This whole setup is designed to support two families."

"Exactly."

"And your dad doesn't see the flaw in that?"

He set the basket on the ground and opened it, pulling out a blanket. "He didn't. He does now."

"Hmm..."

With a quick whip, he unfurled the blanket and let it drift to the rich green grass. "A question?"

She helped him straighten the edges. "No. Probably more of an observation. I wonder if sometimes you don't scare your dad."

He pulled a bottle of grape juice out of the basket and two wineglasses. "Scare my dad?" He chuckled. "I doubt it."

"Oh, I'm sure he wouldn't let you see it. But he'd have to be blind not to realize how much you do…how far ahead you can think."

He shrugged, placed the basket in the middle of the blanket and motioned for her to sit. "Perhaps."

She lowered herself to the spot across from him. "No *perhaps* about it. I'd be willing to bet a year's salary he's waiting for the day you boot him out of the head chair at board meetings."

"Then he doesn't know me well. I respect his position as eldest in his family. As long as he is alive he will be head of our household."

"And you'll run everything discreetly in the background."

He laughed. "It's what I do."

She shook her head. "So maybe it's not as easy having parents as I've always thought."

She made the comment so casually he might have missed it if he hadn't been working to figure out her secrets. Knowing she was a foster child, it wasn't a stretch to understand that she probably longed for a place. So maybe she wanted another job, one with more employees—or maybe fewer employees—where she could build a "work" family. God knew he and Riccardo weren't the two friendliest guys. They were driven. Work oriented. He'd never even as much as asked her to have a drink with him at the end of the day.

Which would have been fruitless anyway, since she didn't drink.

He picked up the bottle of grape juice. "We make this in limited quantities."

She peered at it. "It's not wine?"

"Nope. Just rich, delicious juice."

She laughed. "Always selling."

"That's the other thing I do. I sell. I know how to get people to want what I have."

Her face scrunched. "I never looked at it that way."

"How else do you think you sell? By badgering people?" He batted a hand. "That only turns people off." He caught her gaze. "You need to entice them. Seduce them."

She stiffened ever so slightly and shifted back.

She'd pulled away from him the night before. Not because she didn't want to be seduced, but because she did. He could feel it in her kiss. So now he would go back to selling himself—selling *them*. They might not be a forever match. He had too many responsibilities to be a husband. But there was no reason they couldn't spend time together now. Especially if becoming her lover earned him enough of her trust that she'd tell him her secrets and let him help her.

He took out roast beef sandwiches, cheese and fruit and set them on the blanket between them, then he leaned across his offering, took her small chin in his fingers and brushed his lips over hers quickly, briefly, teasing her.

"I hope you like roast beef."

"I do."

He swore he could feel the trembling of her heart in her shivery whisper. Now that she was getting to know him, she liked him. She could no longer hide it and he intended to take full advantage of it.

He handed her a napkin and a plate.

Her eyebrows rose. "The good china?"

He shrugged. "Maybe. I just told the chef to put in nice plates."

"They're pretty."

He laughed at her attempt to change the subject and brought it back to where he wanted it. "A man doesn't seduce a woman with paper plates." He motioned to the cheese and fruit platter. "Go on. Eat."

She ran her tongue along her lips and the thrill of victory raced through Mitch's blood. He could take her right here. Right now. But he wanted to do this correctly. Short term didn't mean shortchange. Their affair would be passionate. Perfect.

He poured the juice, handed a glass to her. "Have you ever tried wine?"

Her gaze shot to his. Everything he'd done that day had begun to weave a connection between them. So he could seduce her. She wasn't so in-experienced that she didn't see that, and a hum had started in her heart and radiated out to every part of her. Not because the man of her crush suddenly wanted her. But because the Mitch she was getting to know—the nice guy, the strong man who took over his family business without deposing his dad, the man who loved his nanna and went to extraordinary lengths to make sure the brother who stole his girlfriend had a good wedding—because *that* guy wanted her.

"No. I've never tried wine."

"Maybe tonight?" He smiled. His lips tipped up. His eyes filled with warmth. He wanted her to share something that was important to him.

Temptation crept up on her. Not in a bad way, but as a curiosity. Her entire life had been lived waiting for the day she would find her mom, rebuild her family. Now, realizing that dream wouldn't happen, everything was open to her. Was it so wrong to want a real relationship with Mitch? To share his world? The product he was so proud of? If she tried all the things she'd stayed away from, would she actually find herself? Her real self?

She closed her eyes, pulled in a breath. She'd never been more real than she was in that moment. She was on a blanket with a man she was growing to love. Not for his looks. Not for his money. Not for some stupid daydream. But for him. And like it or not, she had a past. She couldn't pretend she didn't. Couldn't pretend she could drink wine and act as if nothing mattered.

Who she was at this very second was real Lila. And if he wanted her, he had to take all of her.

When she opened her eyes, she said, "I don't drink because my mother is an alcoholic."

Mitch's face scrunched in confusion. "Your mother was an alcoholic?"

"My mother *is* an alcoholic. She's alive, I think, living in New York City. I was taken away from her when I was ten. Before I started working with you, I'd been trying to find her."

"*That's* why you don't drink?"

She nodded. "Alcoholism can be inherited. I spent too many horrible days and nights as a child to risk it."

* * *

Even though she made it all sound so simple, a million things bombarded Mitch's brain. She'd been raised by foster parents, taken away from her mom, probably because of her mom's drinking. He knew that had to be part of why she didn't want to talk about her time in foster care. Other kids in her situation didn't have parents. She'd had one who hadn't been able to care for her and had lost custody.

Had she longed for her mom? Wished her mom would sober up? Been disappointed a million times?

What a horrible childhood that must have been.

His heart hurt for her. He balanced his glass on the lid of the picnic basket so he could put his hands on her shoulders. They drifted down along her arms, soothing her. "I'm so sorry."

"You asked me once if I'd ever done anything stupid. Well, I have. When I was ten I told the social worker that my mom slept a lot. I showed her an empty whiskey bottle I'd pulled from the trash. She put it all together and within twenty-four hours I was in a foster home."

*And she blamed herself.*

He didn't believe it was possible to feel any worse for her, but here he was stunned and aching for her. His hands slid from her forearms to her fingers. He caught them up and squeezed.

"That must have been awful."

She met his gaze. "Do you know how horrible it is to feel like you did something terribly, terribly wrong when you were only trying to protect yourself?"

His feelings worsened. Not only had she lost her mom and blamed herself, but there was an ache to it. She had been a scared, maybe hungry child, trying to protect herself and instead she'd lost her mom.

He shook his head. "I'm so sorry you went through that." He tried to reconcile beautiful Lila sitting beside him with mousy Lila who had worked for him for a year and little Lila who had lost her mom, and suddenly everything about her made sense. She didn't accent her beauty or call attention to herself in any way because the last time she had, she'd lost the most important thing in her world. Her mom.

But even as he thought that, he realized something else. She might have been taken away from her mom, but she hadn't actually lost her permanently.

He squeezed her hands again. "So your mom is alive? In New York?"

She pulled in a breath and caught his gaze with her pale gray eyes. "The last I heard, she was alive. But I don't know where she is. Private investigators cost more than I can afford for a sustained period of time. It seems that when I hire one who finds her, she somehow disappears."

He almost couldn't bear to hear that, didn't want to process it, but he had to. While she was talking to him, he also had to be brutally honest. "Do you think she doesn't want you to contact her?"

"I didn't think that." She caught his gaze. "Until I came here. Met your family." She shrugged and looked away. "I don't know. Somehow it all came together in my head. That a mom who wanted me in her life wouldn't run every time I found her."

And it was killing her. Grasping for straws, he said, "Maybe she's still drinking? Maybe she doesn't want you to see her like that? Or maybe she believes *you* wouldn't want *her* in your life?"

Her spine stiffened. "She might have trouble acclimating or she might be finding better jobs, better places to live, pulling herself up by her bootstraps. Improving her life. I know that's not easy. But when someone spends money to find you, you have to know she wants you in her life."

His chest filled with sadness. "I suppose."

She said, "Don't feel bad. It took me three days before the truth sank in. But it's in and I'm okay with it."

She might be resigned, but he felt awful. Well and truly awful. *This* was why she hadn't wanted to talk about her past. It was also why she wanted a job with more money. She'd wanted to find her mom. But being with his family had forced her to face the truth that maybe her mom didn't want her.

He looked around at the two vineyards that made up his family's estate. Rolling hills. Grapevines. Houses. Limos. A jet.

She probably thought the entire Ochoa clan was spoiled, selfish, except for Nanna. She probably also had no idea how her story had affected him. Broken his heart for her. But he suspected that if she knew he felt sorry for her it would make her angry.

The sound of an ATV drowned out the *swish, swish, swish* of the grapevine leaves shivering in the breeze. His head snapped up and he peered at the vehicle, trying to figure out the driver. When he realized it was Julia, he had to stifle a groan.

She roared her ATV up to their blanket. "Here you are!"

Tired of her antics and bad timing, he said, "What do you want, Julia?"

"I think your fiancée forgot the bachelorette party I planned."

"For yourself? You planned your own bachelorette party?"

She smiled prettily. "I had to make sure I got

what I wanted. So I told the girls to leave it to me." She looked at Lila. "But you were gone when we came to pick you up."

Mitch started to say, "She's busy right now."

But Lila touched his arm to stop him, as she addressed Julia. "Drive me back. Give me ten minutes to change and we can go."

Always happy to get her own way, Julia beamed.

Lila gave him a sad smile. "You don't mind gathering all this stuff up by yourself."

He studied her face. Knew she was leaving because what she'd told him had been difficult for her and the outcome hadn't been what either had expected.

Because whether he liked admitting it or not, her past had a bearing on their future. When he boiled it all down, what he wanted from Lila was a few months, maybe a year of fun. Selfish to be sure. But that's who he was.

As pretty as she was, as fun as she was, as much as he was attracted to her, she was wounded. Truly wounded. She'd endured a level of pain, hurt and emptiness that a man like him would only intensify.

He couldn't have her. Not even for a few months. Not even once.

He reached for the wineglasses. "Go. Have fun." Then he smiled at her. "Spend money."

# CHAPTER ELEVEN

MITCH DIDN'T KNOW where they had gone for the bachelorette party, but at six he showered to get ready to go to his brother's bachelor party. If he looked at the situation with Lila closely, she'd been warning him off all along, and he'd been too stupid or maybe too arrogant to heed her.

Because he was a fixer, he believed he could fix anything.

But how could he fix a lifetime of loneliness and guilt? A mom who probably didn't want her? He couldn't.

It was no wonder she didn't want him in her life.

Still, a little after seven, when he heard his apartment door open, he raced out to the sitting room hoping it was her, only to find Riccardo.

"I thought we were meeting at seven?"

Mitch glanced at his watch. Twenty after. "I

wasn't quite ready." He'd been stalling for time. Hoping she'd come back. Why? He had absolutely no clue. There was nothing he could say to her. Nothing he could do to make her life better. He should stay out of it. With his track record with women, he'd undoubtedly end up making her pain worse.

Ducking into his bedroom, he grabbed his wallet. "But I'm ready now."

He, Riccardo, Alonzo and six of Alonzo's friends piled into the limo and headed into town. Mitch had no idea where they were going. If this were New York, they'd go to a strip club. But it wasn't New York. It was rural Spain. Their choices were limited.

Alonzo opened the limo bar, which had obviously been stocked for the occasion.

Riccardo hooted with laughter. "Shots?"

A general cry of agreement from Alonzo's friends followed.

Mitch cringed. But when they handed him a shot glass, he took it. He was, after all, the best man. "What is this?"

Riccardo raised his glass in a toast. "The finest tequila money can buy."

"So we're not going to take our time getting drunk? We're going straight to the trouble."

Alonzo playfully punched his arm. "This is my last hurrah. I want it."

Riccardo said, "To Alonzo. And a long, happy marriage after a wicked night in Monaco."

Mitch raised his shot to drink, but what Riccardo said settled in at the same time that he realized they weren't going to town when the limo turned left. He squeezed his eyes shut. "We're going to the airstrip."

Riccardo laughed. "Well, we're sure as hell not going to drive to Monaco."

No. He supposed they couldn't.

And he should also stop being so morose. This was his brother getting married—to Mitch's ex-girlfriend. Did he want to ruin all the progress they'd made with the charade and have Alonzo's friends think he was upset about Alonzo marrying Julia?

He grabbed the tequila bottle and refilled everyone's glass. "One more. A toast to my brother and his bride-to-be that they will have a houseful of kids."

Alonzo laughed. "Julia might not be on board with that."

Mitch shrugged. "So?"

One of Alonzo's friends said, "And *that's* why you lost her."

Everybody laughed, but Riccardo quickly picked up the charade and said, "But he found an even more beautiful woman."

Chuck Martin, one of Alonzo's childhood friends, said, "Lila is something."

Alonzo nodded. "At first, I thought she was a bit stiff. But she really loosened up when you were dancing the other night. And I totally saw why you love her." He winked. "Besides her good looks."

Uncomfortable, Mitch held up his hands. "Are we going to sit here and talk about my fiancée like a bunch of old women? Or are we going to drink?"

They downed the shot Mitch had poured and

Chuck grabbed the bottle, pouring another round. They toasted Alonzo and Julia again and again, until the next shot Mitch secretly spilled into a nearby wastebasket.

With a designated driver and probably hotel rooms booked, he shouldn't have cared if he got drunk. But as the feeling of the alcohol taking him began to slither through Mitch, he thought of Lila. About how she didn't drink. About how her mother had been a drunk. And the whole ritual of getting plastered seemed wrong. He could see the value of a nice glass of wine. Maybe a sipping whiskey. But to drink for the purpose of getting drunk…

It had more than lost its luster.

The drive to the airstrip took forty minutes. By the time they got there, the light of the sun was weak and shimmery, and Alonzo, his groomsmen and his friends were singing off-color songs. They rolled out of the limo and, arms on each other's shoulder, they headed for the stack of steps leading into the Ochoa family jet.

Mitch stared at them as they disappeared into

the plane. A minute passed. Then two. But he couldn't seem to get his feet moving toward the steps. He glanced at Fernando, the family's long-time driver. One of Fernando's eyebrows rose, then he opened the limo door again.

Mitch laughed.

"I'm sure, Señor Ochoa, that they won't even notice you aren't there."

Another laugh burst from Mitch. "You're probably right."

"So go home. Go see the pretty girl they talked about."

He shouldn't. Lila probably wanted a break from him. And he now felt odd being around her. Spoiled. More selfish than he'd ever thought he was.

"She's at the bachelorette party."

Fernando shrugged. "So maybe you just take a little time to yourself."

That sounded amazing. Since he'd gotten to Spain he'd attended ten meetings about the family business. He'd entertained Lila, watched out for Lila, kept Lila on track. And then there were the family dinners, family breakfasts, balls, garden parties...

He was tired. Not just tired of being on, but maybe he was tired of being all things to all people.

He got into the limo.

He spent the forty-minute drive back to Ochoa Vineyards with his eyes closed and his head resting on the seat. When the limo pulled up to the duplex, he felt marginally better. He got out, joked with Fernando a bit, then climbed the stairs to his apartment. He would get out of this suit, into something comfortable, and read a book.

But when he opened the apartment door, he stopped dead in his tracks. Lila sat on the sofa in the sitting room. Wearing sweatpants, her big shirt and her glasses, she sat cross-legged, watching television.

He tossed his wallet to the door by the table. "Television?"

She flicked off the TV. "I was bored."

"So what happened to Julia's bachelorette party?"

"We went to a spa in town. Got massages. Got makeovers." She presented her fingernails to him. "And manicures."

"At least you didn't have eight shots of tequila."

She winced. "They were about to go barhopping when I bowed out."

"Smart."

"Yeah."

The conversation died a natural death and Mitch glanced around nervously. He wanted a minute to himself, and instead he found the one person he didn't want to see. The one person he should stay away from. Because he didn't want to hurt her.

"I guess I'll go to bed."

"At nine?"

"I was going to read."

"That makes sense."

Awkward silence filled the room again.

She pulled in a breath. "You know what? I think I'm going out to the balcony to look at the moon."

The urge to join her fluttered through him. There was nothing like the sight of the moon rising over the mountains and above the vineyard. He struggled to keep himself from saying, "I think I'll come too."

When they weren't knee-deep in the charade, he liked being in her company. She was normal. Funny. And so easy to be with, she was exactly what he needed after ten days of talking business and forty minutes with friends getting drunk.

But, in the end, he reminded himself that she was a nice woman. And he was—well, him.

He walked into his bedroom, slipped out of his shirt and trousers and into sweatpants and a T-shirt, very much like what she was wearing.

He opened the drapes on the French doors in his room, telling himself it was an easy, nonintrusive way to get a glimpse of the moon. But he knew it was actually his curiosity about Lila that had him looking at the balcony. Seeing her out there alone, watching the great yellow ball, his heart filled to bursting. He might not be right for her. She might not be right for him to have a fling with, but she was alone and he couldn't stand seeing her alone.

He walked out, sat on the chaise beside hers,

stretching out his legs and relaxing on the long chair, and silently watched the moon with her.

"I've seen the moon in New York City."

He laughed at the easy way she started a conversation. "Yeah. I figured you had."

"I'm not totally deprived, you know. In fact, I'm normally a very happy person."

He glanced over at her. Moonlight picked up the yellow in her hair and made it shine. Her gray eyes were serious, intent, so he answered seriously. "Yeah. I get that."

"I don't want you feeling sorry for me."

"I know *that* too."

"Don't get snooty. I'm allowed a little pride."

He sniffed. "Huh. You have a lot of pride."

"Coming from the king of pride, I'm not sure if that's an honest observation or just you trying to find similarities between us."

"We have a lot in common."

She glanced around the estate, then burst into giggles. "Right."

He sat up on the chaise, facing her, and forced her gaze to his. "You think we don't? We're both driven. We both respect family. You might not have your mom in your life, but you respect her. And we don't go out of our way to make ourselves the center of attention like Julia and Alonzo. We're happy in the background. Doing things. Making things happen."

Her head tilted. "Wow. We're practically twins."

"Is that how you handle life? When something pops up that you don't want to discuss you make a joke of it?"

She shrugged. "I don't know. Maybe."

He blinked. "I expected you to dodge that question."

"Ech. I'm not in a dodging mood."

His heart flipped. The moon illuminated the vineyard. The gentle *swish, swish, swish* of grape leaves blowing in the breeze sang through the air. And the woman he was growing to believe he might love wasn't in the mood to dodge his questions.

He turned and settled on the chaise again. Relaxed. Closed his eyes, wondering what he should ask her.

What he should tell her.

And wondering why the very thought of an honest conversation with her made him happier than he'd been in years.

Lila settled on her chaise. All along Mitch had been showing her pieces of the real him. Especially dancing. Just the thought of how much fun they had shot a thrill of memory through her. They'd danced. They kissed. They'd told each other secrets. After ten days, she was probably closer to him than she'd ever been to anyone. Even Sally. Because there were things she didn't think Sally could handle that she knew Mitch could.

"My first summer vacation was actually a shopping trip."

He glanced over at her. "Really?"

"Most foster families provide things like clothes but don't take you shopping. So this one year, my foster mom could see I was bored. I tried to hide it. I tried to pretend it wasn't true. But she saw right through me. I'd never said anything but I think somehow she knew I'd never been shopping for real. I'd looked in store windows and walked up and down the aisles of stores just to see what was there. But I'd never shopped." She smiled. "She taught me about clearance racks."

He laughed.

"She also took me shopping every other month. There wasn't a lot of money to spend on clothes. But it was nice—special—not just that she spent the time with me but that she let me have choices."

He nodded. "I would have shot myself if my mom had expected me to pick out my own clothes."

She laughed. "We're not sounding so much the same anymore, are we?"

He batted a hand. "We're still the same in the things that count."

"You don't think being raised in the lap of luxury and being raised to count pennies makes us different?"

"No. Because I think we ended up with the same core values."

"Interesting."

"Not really. I was in university when I began to see there were too many of us to be supported by the vineyard. In a way, that was my first experience of counting pennies."

"Except your pennies were dollars."

"It's still money."

They were quiet for a minute, then he said, "Julia never got that."

"I don't think Julia wanted to get it."

He shrugged. "Maybe."

"How'd you ever end up with her anyway?"

"My relationship with Julia was almost an accident. We went to the same school as kids, went to the same parties. We just sort of evolved."

"So you were with her for *years*? You'd never dated anybody else?"

"There's a lot to be said for convenience and comfort."

She winced. "I'll bet Julia would love hearing that."

He laughed. "When we broke up, I went a little crazy dating in New York."

"You don't have to confess all that to me."

"You need to know who I am. That I'm a bit selfish. And I have tunnel vision. I will do whatever I have to do to keep my family safe, happy, pampered."

He was telling her not to make anything of this. Maybe because the conversation had given him the same warm feeling of connection that it was giving her and he didn't want it? Whatever the reason, she respected his wishes and wouldn't force him to say the obvious. She knew, as all good foster kids knew, how to turn the conversation in a neutral direction.

"They're very lucky to have you."

He waited a beat. Then he shifted on his chaise again so that he was facing her. "And your mom would be very lucky to have you. God only knows what kinds of demons she's facing, what kind of life she has. You can't judge her or assume any of her motivations. You can only make your life the best it can be."

Tears welled in her eyes, but she stopped them. What kind of guy warns you off in one breath and soothes your soul in the next.

"Spoken like a man who's figured the same thing about himself."

"I have to keep my family solvent." He rose.

Tired, ready to give up her star/moon gazing for the night, she rose too.

"And I have a good life."

Standing in front of him, a little shorter than he was without her three-inch heels, she whispered, "I have a good life too."

"Then neither of us has anything to complain about... *Si?*"

Right at that moment, she could think of at least one thing. His dedication to his family would keep him on a solitary path. At the same time that she envied him for his family, his destiny, she suddenly felt cheated. That moment she'd been thinking about since she talked to Sally... This was it. And he was telling her he didn't want it.

She rose to her tiptoes. She wasn't trying to change his mind. She wasn't trying to make a point. She just wanted to kiss him. If this ache of understanding and connection was love, no matter if he was turning it down, she wanted at least a kiss.

She touched his mouth with hers, softly, gently, as she slid her hands up his arms and to his shoulders. At first, she thought he'd refuse her, but suddenly his hands came to her shoulders and slid to her nape, forcing his fingers into the thick locks of her hair, sending tingles of joy down her spine.

She stretched higher to deepen the kiss and he bent a bit so that their mouths could meet and merge, as if he was unable to stop himself.

And that was the moment she didn't just know she loved him. She also knew he loved her.

# CHAPTER TWELVE

MITCH FELL INTO the kiss. Drowning in sensation, he pressed his mouth to hers, even as he grazed his hands down her back, forcing her body as close to his as he could possibly get it. She was warm. She was wonderful. But more than that she was the first person to really know him. Him. Quirks. Foibles. Destiny and all.

Knowing someone completely was the only way anyone could really love anyone else. Now she knew him. And he knew her.

And it was pointless.

Because he really didn't want to hurt her. As pretty as she was, as fun as she was, as much as he was attracted to her, she came with baggage. Real pain and hurt and emptiness. At some point, he'd only make her life worse.

He pulled away, slid his hands up her back to

her shoulders and to her face, as he stared into her eyes. For one blistering minute, he longed to throw caution to the wind. To tell her she was perfect and he wanted her. Then he heard the sounds of the limo returning. He heard Julia's laugh as she got out of the limo so she could clamber to the house she shared with Alonzo, and he pulled back. Julia had dumped him because he was never there for her.

Lila needed somebody who would be there for her.

She didn't need him.

A few years from now she would thank him for stepping away from her, saying "Good night" and returning to his room alone.

The next morning, Mitch had himself all together. He hadn't spent a sleepless night. He'd thought it all through and fixed it.

He'd always known he had tunnel vision. After Julia, he'd realized he wasn't made to be a one-woman man. But what he had forgotten was that he'd promised Lila a job. When he remembered that, the fixer in him had perked up like a bull seeing a red flag. He might not be able to love her, but he could help her.

So he'd made a few calls to friends in New York, and because it was still afternoon in the States, within hours he had the perfect job for Lila.

Then he realized that there was an even better way to repay her for helping him with this ruse. For being a good sport. For being a nice person. She needed a job, but she also wanted to find her mom. She wanted the chance at a family that he'd always had and maybe taken for granted.

Because it wasn't quite five o'clock in New York City, the town was still open for business. He pulled a few strings and got the name of a private investigator. With the promise of a bonus for quick work, he hired a firm that began looking for Lila's mom. He didn't ask what websites they'd checked, if they'd hacked things that shouldn't be hacked, but two hours later he not only had her mom's employer; he had her address and phone number.

Then he slept like a baby.

\* \* \*

Sitting at the far end of the conference table, listening to his dad convene the final meeting of his stay in Spain, he felt pretty damned proud of himself. His family was solvent. The woman he might be coming to love would have a secure future once he told her about the job he'd found for her. She'd also have another shot at talking to her mom.

And he was back to being who he was. Not the needy man standing on the balcony wondering if he should take a risk.

He hated risk. Even considering taking a risk was foolish. Not him. And he was glad to be back to normal.

"As most of you have probably guessed, we have no agenda for this final meeting because there's nothing left to discuss."

Though everyone else in the conference room laughed, Mitch struggled to keep his facial expression neutral. He could be in his apartment right now, telling Lila she had a high-level administrative position in an investment bank and handing her mom's personal information to her. Instead, he would sit here and listen to his dad rehash decisions that had already been made.

But he could do it. He was Mitch Ochoa, fixer, background guy who made other people happy.

"But there is one thing we haven't discussed."

There might be. But Mitch honestly had no clue what it was.

"I'd like to acknowledge my son…"

Alonzo. Who was getting married.

"Mitcham."

For a few seconds his name didn't register. When it did, he glanced up sharply.

"You think the family doesn't see that you rescued us. But we do. Alonzo will be a great vintner. Your mother and aunt love managing the restaurant and gift shops. I'm okay with overseeing everybody. But, you, Mitch, fill in the final piece of the puzzle. The big piece. You sell us. Without you, we'd be broke."

He sat back in his chair. Not quite sure what to say.

Riccardo laughed. "He hates praise."

"I don't hate praise. I simply don't need praise."

"It's a foolish family," his mom said, "who doesn't acknowledge the person who's holding it all together."

"I wouldn't say that I—"

Riccardo snorted. "Oh, please. Modesty? Take the praise and run."

"Better yet," his dad suggested. "Take a vacation. We've looked at the books and we've never seen that you take time off."

Because he didn't.

His mom reached across the conference table and patted his hand. "We also worry that you don't have a life."

"I have plenty of life."

"True, but I wonder if Lila feels that way." His mom caught his gaze. "Riccardo tells me you've never even taken her to the house in the Hamptons. Your dates are all in New York City. You need to give this woman more."

Oh, boy. Dating advice. From his mom.

Here's where he had to stop things.

He rose from the table. "Okay. Good talk. I'll

just be going back to my apartment now." He started to turn away, but shifted back. "In fact, I'll take your advice, and Lila and I will have lunch in town."

Before he could make his escape, his dad walked over to him and gave him a stiff, all-businessman hug. "I'm still the boss, but I wanted you to know that we see what you do." He pulled away and caught Mitch's gaze. "I know you saved us financially, but we've all agreed this week that we're on solid ground now. You can go and have some fun."

Mitch left the conference room and all but ran out of the main house. But when he got to the sitting room of his apartment and saw Lila on the sofa reading, he stopped dead in his tracks. His family had given him the green light to slow down, take time off.

What if he did?

What if, after the wedding, he and Lila got into the family jet and toured Europe?

The possibility was so tempting his breath almost caught. He could have or do anything he wanted and what he wanted was time with this woman.

Except he wasn't a guy who could make commitments. And he would hurt her.

She looked up and saw him. "Hey."

"Hey."

She turned off her e-reader. "Sorry, I was a little lost in my story. How'd the meeting go?"

She rose from the sofa. Her long legs seemed to go on forever beneath her short shorts. Her hair swayed as she walked over to him. And her soft eyes called to him.

"The meeting was fine."

"So what's on the agenda for today?"

He fingered the slip of paper in his jacket pocket. The name and address of the company for her new job. The address and phone number for her mom.

"My dad told me today, in front of everyone, that he realizes I saved the family."

Her eyebrows rose. "That's cool."

Now that he was past the dating advice and remembering the things his dad had said, it was cool. Warmth bubbled up in his chest. All the weird feelings from the unexpected praise disappeared like a puff of smoke. The sense of accomplishment that rippled through him made him laugh.

"It was great. A surprise, but great. I think my dad might be making a road for a new way for the family's company to do business."

He fell to the sofa, happily confused.

"And that's good too, right?"

"Absolutely."

No feeling had ever come close to the emotions rolling through him at that moment. Another man might have looked at Lila, with his family's instructions for him to have some fun floating through his brain, and seen his chance. Mitch remembered that he wasn't a good bet as a boyfriend and Lila needed more.

And suddenly everything felt off. Wrong.

They had three more days of this charade. Three days of getting to know her, laughing with her, longing for something he couldn't have.

Maybe it was time for this ruse to end? His

family respected him. He'd found her mom. They both had what they wanted.

Except he wanted her.

But he couldn't have her. It annoyed him that his usual self-control was deserting him. When he decided against something, he never thought of it again. He didn't torture himself. He took action.

He rose from the sofa. "I found you a job."

Her eyes widened. "You did?"

The excitement in her voice strengthened his resolve. He hadn't even told her about her mom yet, but she was so thrilled with the job it was clear she wasn't invested in this, in him, the way he was beginning to feel about her.

He reached into his pocket and pulled out the little slip of paper. "Your mom's address and phone number are on there too."

Her mouth fell open. "Oh, my God."

She was just about to jump in his arms and tell him she loved him, when he said, "I found your mom because I don't like to do things halfway. I realized last night that you wanted your mom, not a job. So I did what I should have done in the beginning—I hired a PI and found her. The new job is like a bonus as a thank-you for being so convincing as my fiancée."

She stepped back, away from him so she could see his face. He'd said the words as if he was happy, proud of himself, but she saw deeper. She saw the flicker of uncertainty in his eyes.

"You found my mom last night?"

He nodded. "It was only afternoon in New York City, even after our chat on the balcony."

When she'd kissed him.

And he'd pulled away.

He'd immediately gone to his room and found her mom.

She took another step back.

He might have feelings for her. She'd sure as hell felt them the night before. But he didn't want to love her.

Her heart felt crushed. Not smashed into a million pieces, but flattened into a thin red line.

And she still had to go to the rehearsal dinner

that night, pretending everything was okay. Then the wedding. The day-after party.

She had to. He'd done his side of the deal. Found her a job. Then gone the extra mile and found her mom.

She had to.

Her heart tried to swell back to life, but couldn't. She was right at his fingertips. He loved her. But he wouldn't say it. Didn't want her.

When the chips were down, when commitments had to be made, no one really wanted her.

She cleared her throat to ease the tears out of her voice. "You do remember that my mom always disappears right after she's found." The right thing to do would be stay and finish this. But with every ounce of her being she knew she couldn't.

Gathering her courage, she raised her eyes to look at him. "I can't wait on this." She waved the paper. "I have to return to America today."

For one blessed second, he hesitated. Hope swelled, but he dashed it. "I don't think we have to go through with the rest of the charade."

She blinked, the tears a little harder to hold back this time.

"My family respects me." He nodded at the paper in her hands. "We found your mom. We accomplished everything we wanted."

Nodding, she swallowed hard to hold back the emotion flooding through her. *She'd* wanted her association with him to be over when she returned to New York. She'd known it was the only way she could handle this.

But now that the time was here…

Her chest shuddered with unshed tears and she pressed her lips together to settle herself before she said, "You're right. Give me an hour or so to pack. You can think of a good breakup story for your family."

He nodded.

She straightened her shoulders and walked into her bedroom.

# CHAPTER THIRTEEN

LILA ARRIVED IN New York feeling like a new person. Unfortunately, it wasn't the new person she'd thought she'd be when she agreed to the charade with Mitch.

She thought she'd come back with four suitcases of beautiful clothes, a sophisticated knowledge of Spain and how the other half lives and a new job she could sink her teeth into. Though she had those, she'd brought home something else with her.

She was truly in love with Mitch. And she knew he loved her too. But he'd nudged her out because he didn't *want* to love her. Who knew why? On the flight home she'd wondered if he didn't think her good enough, but recognized that wasn't true. He wasn't that kind of guy. She'd considered that what had blossomed between them had happened too fast. But he didn't have to ask her to marry him. They could have dated.

He didn't even want to give them a chance.

And she had to deal with that. Straight up. No pulling punches. The man had had her at his fingertips, and he'd given her the one thing he knew would push her away—her mom.

But somehow having her mom's address felt empty. Worse, it was frightening. She'd turned her mom in. Who knew how she'd react? What would she do if her mom didn't run this time, but stayed and talked with her, and flat out told her she didn't want her in her life. Then she would have been rejected by her mom and the man she loved.

Then it would be official. There would be no one in the world more alone than she was.

The next morning, Mitch woke and stumbled into the kitchen of his apartment. The one bad thing about being with a woman who had a good reason not to drink was he now couldn't get drunk to drown his sorrows. He looked at alcohol a to-tally different way now.

So he'd barely slept. And he hadn't had the sweet release of alcoholic oblivion to get him through the night. Instead, he'd gone back and forth between thinking he was an idiot and know-ing he'd had to do the right thing.

His wedding tux hung on a rack in his sitting room—obviously delivered by staff. He wasn't shaved. He didn't feel like showering. He drank coffee but he'd just as soon throw the bagel at the wall as eat it.

A knock at his door surprised him. Thinking it was someone here to annoy him with some detail about the wedding, he barked, "Come in!"

The door opened slowly and Julia entered. "A best man is supposed to attend all wedding func-tions, including the rehearsal dinner, so where were you last night?"

"Taking my fiancée to the airstrip." He tossed the bagel to the table. "We broke up." And it felt real. And it sucked. And it confused the hell out of him. All the time he'd been trying to avoid hurting her, and he was the one hurting.

Julia's face fell in confusion. "You broke up?"

"Don't pretend you're not happy. Now you're back to being queen bee. I know you didn't like her."

"I adored her. She was the first person to hold her own with me in a long time. But honestly I knew something was up when she left the bachelorette dinner. I knew you were going to do something stupid."

"Yeah, well, the stupid thing I did was find her mother."

Julia fell to the seat across from his at the small, round table. "Her mother?"

"She wasn't in foster care because she was an orphan. Her mother is alive. She lost custody when Lila was about ten. Lila hasn't seen her since. Every time she finds her mom, she disappears. It seems she likes her mother more than she likes me. Because as soon as I gave her her mom's address she was out of here." That wasn't quite the truth. Though she'd been the first to mention leaving, he'd agreed.

"And she gave you back the ring?"

He ran his hand along the back of his neck. "No."

"Maybe you misinterpreted? You did say her mom disappears every time she's found. Maybe Lila didn't think she could wait."

"That was part of it, but I... Never mind."

"Never mind like hell. You love this woman! Are you just going to let her go?"

"She's better off without me."

"No. She's not! *I* was," she said, then she grinned. "But that's because you didn't love me. You could drop me for a business meeting any day of the week. But you're different with her. You sometimes can't take your eyes off her. She knows enough about business that you talk for real." She smiled. "You take her seriously, Mitch. And she makes you laugh. You love her."

Julia rose and took his tux off the rack. "You need to go after her."

"After her?"

"Are you deaf or daft? First off, you're sending her to meet her mom alone. My goodness, Mitch. Seriously? She hasn't seen her mother in over fifteen years and you sent her into that emotional land mine alone?"

He'd never thought of that. It should have shamed him that self-absorbed Julia had. "I'm not sure what I'm supposed to do."

"Nothing…just support her. Be moral support." She tapped his forearm. "She needs you, Mitch. And you love her. Go."

"What about your best man?"

"Riccardo will fill in." She waved the tux. "Luckily, you're the same size."

Lila sat at her kitchen table, staring at the piece of paper with her mom's address and phone number on it. Mitch had found her mom. She had the information about her new job. She'd already called and learned that she could start the following Monday. She had three closets full of clothes and a ring the size of a small town on her finger. She was going to have to return the ring—in person—only a fool would put a ring this valuable in the mail. But she couldn't seem to move from the table.

Oh, she wanted her mom. She longed for the chance to say she was sorry, to make things right, but she also wanted Mitch. Everything she'd resolved to avoid when she'd made this deal had happened. They'd gotten close. She'd fallen in love for real. He'd fallen for her too, but that stubborn Spanish businessman could not let go and say he wanted her.

So maybe she was better off with a fresh start. Really.

She showered and put on a pair of jeans and one of her new blouses, along with new shoes. She took the subway to the part of town where her mom lived, but walking up the sidewalk, she saw a limo.

She almost laughed. A limo. In this part of town. She thanked God for the laugh since she was shaking in her new shoes. She'd already been rejected by Mitch. Now her mom would probably reject her too. She was the stupidest woman in the world to put herself in these kinds of positions. But if there was even a chance her mother wanted her in her life, she had to do this.

Trembling knees and all.

As she approached the limo, the back window lowered...

"Hey."

Her heart stumbled. Her breath stopped. All thought of her mother disappeared. "Mitch?"

"*Sí.*"

What the hell? The surreal feeling of everything being out of place washed over her and made her dizzy. Then her ring caught the light and bounced it back at her and she understood what was going on.

"You forgot to take back the ring. Is that why you followed me?"

"I know you still have the ring. But that's not why I'm here. Julia doesn't think you should see your mom alone."

Confusion bubbled up again. The whole situation felt like one of those crazy dreams where nothing made sense. "Julia?"

"Julia and I." The limo door opened. He stepped out. "We had a small chat the morning of the wedding and she reminded me how hard this might be for you."

"You talked about me on her wedding day?"

"She let me out of my commitment to be the best man. But we both forgot I'd have to wait for the jet to return to Spain." He laughed. "So I got my tux back from Riccardo and did my duty. And now I'm here. With you." He pointed at the aging town house door. "To meet your mom."

It still didn't quite sink in. "You're coming with me?"

"Yes. Lila, this is a huge deal for you." He shook his head. "I can't imagine how I'd feel right now if I hadn't seen my mom in over a decade." He caught her hands. "I know the story. I know you feel she hates you. How could you think you can face this alone?"

The thought that he could do something so sweet and yet refuse to love her filled her with unbearable sadness. "I've faced everything in my life alone."

"Not this."

Tears pooled in her eyes. How could he not see that having him pop into her life, even for something important, only hurt her? "You don't have to do this."

"That's the beauty of love."

Her head snapped up.

"I get to do all kinds of things I wouldn't ordinarily do." He paused, smiled. "Because I love you."

Her lower lip trembled. She had the sudden, urgent sense that this couldn't be real. That she had to have misinterpreted. Or that he'd qualify his statement by saying something like "I love you as a friend." "You love me?"

"Apparently more than I ever loved Julia because she sees it."

That she hadn't misinterpreted. She laughed through her tears.

"Come here." Holding her close, he whispered, "I thought I wasn't good for you. That I'd hurt you. But when I thought I was fighting feelings for you, what I was really fighting was changing. Falling in love with you was changing me. I didn't see it until Julia said it." He laughed and hugged her close. "You don't have to worry that I'll hurt you."

She believed him. Everything else in her world suddenly seemed easy.

"If your mom doesn't want you—we will deal with it. Because you will have me...and my mother and dad and Julia and Alonzo, Riccardo and his parents...and Nanna. Especially Nanna."

Tears filled her eyes as indescribable joy filled her heart. She pulled back, caught his gaze. "I love you too."

"It certainly took you long enough to say it."

"Two weeks is hardly—"

But he cut her off with a kiss. A slow, heartfelt *I am in this for real* kiss. She melted into him, knowing that absolutely everything in her life had changed.

All because she couldn't resist him when he'd asked for a favor.

He broke the kiss. "Just one thing, though."

"One thing?"

"Ochoas work for Ochoas. I'll expect you in the office on Monday."

She laughed.

He caught her hand and turned her toward the door of her mom's town house. "Shall we?"

She nodded. "I'm ready."

# EPILOGUE

THE WEDDING TOOK place on a beautiful August day. The vineyard looked spectacular. The sun beat down on vines bursting with red grapes ready to be harvested.

Fixing Lila's veil, Julia sighed. "Alonzo and I should have had an August wedding. It's so pretty today. So special."

Lila turned to her with a smile. "I heard your June wedding was just gorgeous. And I saw the pictures."

"I don't think the pictures did justice to my gown." She turned Lila to the full-length mirror where they both could see the elegant bodice and full georgette crepe skirt of her exquisite gown. Julia turned Lila right then left as Sally fussed with the long train that flowed behind Lila.

"I think you need to stand angled just slightly

to the right to make sure the camera picks up the sparkly embellishments in the skirt."

Sally rose and rolled her eyes. "You're too picky, Julia."

Julia shrugged. Sally and Julia wore identical one-shoulder dresses but Sally's was blue and Julia's a vivid shade of coral.

"I like things to be perfect."

"Well, I think Lila is perfect, just the way she is."

Lila caught Sally's hand. "Thank you."

"I think she's perfect too."

Lila, Julia and Sally all turned toward Lila's mom, who closed the dressing room door behind her. A short woman with strawberry blond hair and a dusting of freckles, she looked so much younger, so much happier than when Lila and Mitch had called on her the year before. Not only had Mitch found her a good apartment, he'd given her a job as the receptionist for Ochoa Online and paid her a large enough salary that she could support herself. Lila had lived with her mom off and on in the past year and they'd gotten to know each other.

Today, dressed in a pretty pink gown, Francine would give her daughter away.

Lila walked over and took her hands. "You look wonderful, Mom."

Francine leaned in and kissed Lila's cheek. "You are amazing."

"No. Just finally figured out who I was."

"Well, Mitch helped," Julia said, fluffing her black hair to make sure it was perfect.

Sally sighed with disgust and put one hand on her hip. "Really? How?"

"Well, he is the one who talked her into pretending to be his fiancée, forcing her to come out of her shell."

Sally caught Lila's gaze. "How much do you tell this woman…and why, for heaven's sake?"

Lila walked over and gave Julia a squeeze. "Because she's my sister-in-law, and she's a lot smarter than you think."

"Thank you!" Julia said, returning Lila's hug. She glanced at her watch. "We need to get going.

The ceremony starts in five minutes. We'll need at least two minutes to get to our staging area."

Sally led the way out the door, followed by Julia. Lila took her mom's hand and together they walked to the small tent behind the rows of seats set up to face the vineyards and the setting sun. Lila and her mom had been instructed at the rehearsal the night before to stay in the tent until they heard the first notes of "Here Comes the Bride."

Lila took a deep breath.

"Nervous?"

Lila grinned at her mom. "Not even slightly." This had been the best year of her life. A year to make amends to her mom, who also made amends to her. A year to really fall in love and be in love with the most wonderful man in the world.

How could she possibly be nervous?

Then the first notes of "Here Comes the Bride" sounded and her stomach filled with butterflies. She pressed her tummy. "Well, I'll be darned. I am just a little nervous."

Her mom laughed. "Come on. Once we get

started up that aisle and you see Mitch, you'll be fine."

They exited the little tent and all eyes turned toward them. Lila sucked in a breath and walked down the aisle, smiling at her guests. People she knew very well now. Family.

They got to the end of the aisle, her mom handed her over to Mitch and the ceremony began.

She promised her life and her fidelity to a man who could be as stubborn and exasperating as he was handsome. He promised his life to her, then he grinned. And she remembered all the reasons she loved him.

The minister announced that he could kiss the bride and he did. With one arm supporting her back he dipped her and kissed her like a man so happy he couldn't get enough. Then he brought her back to her feet, pulled her into a dance hold and together they did a bit of a samba.

The crowd laughed. Mitch grinned and Lila soaked it all in.

Family.

Silliness.

Love.
That was all there really was in life.
All she really wanted.

\* \* \* \* \*

*If you've enjoyed this book,*
*then you won't want to miss*
*A MISTLETOE KISS WITH THE BOSS*
*by Susan Meier.*
*Available now!*

*If you want to read another fake fiancée*
*romance, then be sure to indulge in*
*CONVENIENTLY ENGAGED TO THE BOSS*
*by Ellie Darkins.*